I0548085

WHEN JESUS CAME
TO THE BLACK HILLS
TO DO THE GHOST DANCE
WITH THE SPIRIT
OF SITTING BULL

By

J. Wayne Frye

WHEN JESUS CAME TO THE BLACK HILLS
TO DO THE GHOST DANCE
WITH THE SPIRIT OF SITTING BULL

Catalogue Number: 2018-2453598

ISBN: 978-1-928183-35-8

Fireside Books – Victoria, British Columbia
Part of the Peninsula Publishing Consortium

Welcome to the Black Hills,
Where All Hell is About to Break Lose!
From the Book:

The poor man's air force is a car bomb; the poor man's tank is a bomb-laden truck; the poor man's grenade is a Molotov cocktail. Thus, it is the poor guerrilla fighter who improvises his weapons that is called the terrorist, while the American soldier equipped with superior firepower is a defender of freedom – the freedom for the poor, the ignorant and the manipulated to bow before the privileged class in a society of, by and for the wealthy. This is modern America, where those who never have to answer for their crimes against humanity define justice.

- - - - - - - - - - - - - - - - - -

Reviews:

From Que Magazine: Manhattan private eye, Aaron Adams, is once again called in to assist a modern messiah, but like the Jesus in Matthew 10:34, this messiah has not come to bring peace on the earth but a sword. J. Wayne Frye's previous scintillating Aaron Adams thrillers featuring a rebel calling himself Jesus, *When Jesus Came to Jersey as the Son of Thunder* and *When Jesus Came to Canada to Lead an Indigenous Rebellion*, were tame precursors to this hair-raising adventure that will keep you on the edge of your seat.

- - - - - - - - - - - - - - - - - -

From Library Review: Where does Wayne Frye come up with the mesmerizing ideas for his incredible adventures? The defeat of George Custer and his 7th Cavalry at Little Big Horn was the last great victory of the Sioux Nation, but under the guidance of a modern messiah calling himself Jesus, who is arousing the people of the Pine Ridge Reservation, they are about to resurrect the warrior spirit and once again take on the U.S. government in a battle for their beloved Black Hills.

WHEN JESUS CAME
TO THE BLACK HILLS
TO DO THE GHOST DANCE
WITH THE SPIRIT
OF SITTING BULL
is dedicated to some very special people
in my life.

A special dedication to my cousin, **Tommy Tolbert** and his wife **Jan**. This is a trying time in their lives, and I wish them well in dealing with adversity. Although Tommy, no doubt, will disagree with most of what I say within, our mutual respect allows us to disagree without being disagreeable. Time never dulls the exuberance of shared youth, when it seems the world is much less daunting than the world we have to face as adults.

TO:

H.G. and Charlie - They retired to the sunshine of Palm Springs, but once frolicked in delight at my château high on a hill overlooking the ocean in anticipation of living on Vancouver Island. The days of friendship we shared are treasured by an aging mind that clings to those times that are like fine aged wine, flavoured with the ambrosia of sweet memories.

AND AS ALWAYS, TO MY MUSE
Lynton Viñas

J. Wayne Frye   2

WHEN JESUS CAME TO THE BLACK HILLS TO DO THE GHOST DANCE WITH THE SPIRIT OF SITTING BULL

TABLE OF CONTENTS

Introduction - 7
Until all Men are Truly Equal and
Free from the Tyranny of Greed
Prologue – Part 1 - 13
One of History's Greatest Oppressors
Prologue – Part 2 - 21
You Ain't Seen Nothing Yet
Chapter 1 - 37
Blowing in the Wind
Chapter 2 - 45
Anarchy Glorified
Chapter 3 - 67
You Are Already Dead
Chapter 4 - 89
Justice in a Nation that has None
Chapter 5 - 115
Then You Better Come Well-Armed
Chapter 6 - 127
A Big Dose of Justice
Chapter 7 - 149
We Shall Prevail in the End
Chapter 8 - 171
The Flickering Embers of Age
Chapter 9 - 207
On Your Feet, Not on Your Knees
Chapter 10 - 237
To Hear the Song of Fools
Chapter 11 - 247
They Wind up Being Changed by the Devil
Chapter 12 - 261
No Justice for the Powerless
Chapter 13 - 271
Depth of Depravity
Chapter 14 - 287
Toward His Destiny
Epilogue - 297
As He Thought

J. Wayne Frye

ABOUT THE AUTHOR

Wayne Frye's *Aaron Adams* mysteries, *Girl* series books, *Chablis Louise Chavez* thrillers and *Lynton* adventures have titillated the brains of those who enjoy tales that challenge the mind. His life, like those of the heroes he writes about, has been filled with adventure and excitement. He has been a college hockey coach, university professor, and at one time, the youngest university president in the USA. Called a marketing genius by the *LOS ANGELES TIMES*, he has been a promotional consultant to hockey teams and motion picture companies. He has been cited for his work with inner-city gang children in the Los Angeles area and been active in the anti-globalization movement. He lives in Ladysmith, British Columbia,; Laguna, Philippines and Cape Town, South Africa. He provides satirical political commentary to many Canadian newspapers, and his books on politics have created a great deal of controversy.

<u>Some of the 45 Books by J. Wayne Frye</u>

White Meteors and the Ghost of Sue Ann McGee
Hockey Mania and the Mystery of Nancy Running Elk
Something Evil in the Darkness at Hopkins House
How Hockey Saved a Jew From the Holocaust
The Girl Who Stirred up the Whirlwind
The Girl Who Motivated Murder Most Foul
The Girl Who Said Goodbye for the Last Time
Fall From Apocalypse
Armageddon Now
Worth: Part 1
Worth- Part 2: The Night of Thunder Road
When Jesus Came to Jersey as the Son of Thunder
When Jesus Came to Canada to Lead an Indigenous Rebellion
Lynton Curls Her Hair
Lynton Walks on Water
Lynton and the Vampire at Tagaytay Manor
Lynton Buys a Cell-Phone and Hears the Voice of Doom
Lynton Viñas and Beowulf Perez in the Taal Inferno
Lynton and the Ghosts at the Mansion on Balete Drive
Lynton Viñas: Shadow in the Darkness
Lynton's South African Adventure
Lynton and the Stellenbosch Terror
Lynton, the Karoo Vampire and the Jewells of Omar Bin Abi
Chablis: Avenging Angel for the Forgotten
Chablis and the Terrorist Who Resurrected the Spirit of Che
Chablis and Lynton in the Room of Doom
Pursuit
The Disappearance

J. Wayne Frye

WHEN JESUS CAME TO THE BLACK HILLS
TO DO THE GHOST DANCE
WITH THE SPIRIT OF SITTING BULL

INTRODUCTION
UNTIL All MEN ARE TRULY EQUAL AND
FREE FROM THE TYRANNY OF GREED

Old Buffy said it best years ago
And I just can't let that rhythm go.
She used the Cree word Keshagesh,
For animals that never have enough.
They have greedy-guts and they always
Want more and more and more and more!

Today, you see so many business suits,
Never saw a dollar sign that looked so cute.
Never knew a junkie with a money Jones;
He's singing, "Who's selling Park Place.
Who trading the B and O?
Who's buying Boardwalk?"

J. Wayne Frye   7

WHEN JESUS CAME TO THE BLACK HILLS
TO DO THE GHOST DANCE
WITH THE SPIRIT OF SITTING BULL

These old men they make their dirty deals.
Go in the back room and see what they can steal.
Talk about your beautiful and spacious skies.
It's about uranium; it's about the water rights.
Put Mother Nature on a luncheon plate.
They cut her up and call it real estate.

Want all the resources and all of the land.
They make a war over it: Blow things up for it.
The reservation now is poverty row.
There's something cooking and the lights are low.
Somebody's trying to save our mother earth.
I'm gonna help them with its rebirth.

Ole Columbus, he was looking good,
When he got lost in the neighbourhood,
Garden of Eden right before his eyes.
Now it's all spy ware: it's about what you can get.
Ole brother Midas looking hungry today.
What he can't buy he'll get some other way.

Send in the troopers if the natives resist.
Old, old story boys, that's how you do it boys.
Look at these people; ah, they're on a roll.
Gonna have it all, gonna have complete control.
Want all the resources and all of the land.
They'll break the law for it: Blow things up for it.

When all our champions are off in the war,
That is when the suits began the evil bore.

J. Wayne Frye   8

WHEN JESUS CAME TO THE BLACK HILLS
TO DO THE GHOST DANCE
WITH THE SPIRIT OF SITTING BULL

The corporations rip off here is always on.
Mr. Greed I think your time has come.
We're gonna sing it and pray it
And live it and then say it.

Singing: No, no Keshagesh:
You can't do that no more, (no more, no more)
No, no, no, no Keshagesh
You can't do that no more, (no more, no more)
No, no, no, no Keshagesh
You can't do that no more, (no more, no more)*

*Reinterpretation of No No Keshagesh By Buffy St. Marie
Copyright by Gypsy Boy Music, Inc.

Yes, old Christopher Columbus got lost in the neighbourhood, and the rest is history. A man venerated by America as the discoverer of the country, he has a day celebrated in his honour. However, the truth is that he was no man to be honoured. When he sat foot on what he thought was the East Indies, he named the inhabitants Indians because he thought he had landed in India. Thus began the systematic destruction of a way of life that had endured for thousands of years. He, and his Christian crew, saw these people as savages, and they immediately began attempts to convert these heathens to worship the man who died on the cross for all humankind's sins. These white people saw themselves as superior, but the truth was they were the real heathens. They did not bring enlightenment; they brought the darkness of dogmatic religion that enslaved all to an uncompromising God who demanded submission to his will. The only problem was his will was interpreted by a pack of sanctimonious hypocrites who enslaved minds in orthodoxy that was a prison from which few could ever escape and truly find the freedom to realize the God within us all.

All men seek something that is lacking within, something that will give life purpose. Jesus knew the answer to the riddle of life, but no one wanted to know the truth, no one wanted to see that the search, the quest for meaning was a fruitless journey that only would lead to disappointment. Men simply are and that is it. Jesus had journeyed near and far trying to lift up humanity from the misery of a greed driven world so that each individual would discover the joy of the here and now, not wait for some mystical utopia where the righteous would be issued wings and flutter about in the clouds with sanctified purity among loved ones.

Jesus, in the book *When Jesus Came to Jersey as the Son of Thunder*, tried to lead a rebellion of the oppressed in a small New Jersey town, but the U.S. government and the church decried him as an impostor who was perverting God's word. As usual, anyone who dared question authority was deemed a terrorist. Incarcerated and slated for torture and execution, private eye Aaron Adams came to his rescue and put him on a train to Canada. A few years later, Jesus appeared on an island in the Broughton Archipelago off the coast of Vancouver Island, and led a small band of First Nations people in a rebellion against greed by a government hell-bent on exploiting the natural resources of a pristine land. That adventure was detailed in another book aptly named *When Jesus Came to Canada to Lead an Indigenous Rebellion in the Broughton Archipelago.*

Now Jesus was once again stirring up trouble, in of all places, the sanctified and hallowed place known as Wounded Knee. How this extraordinary occurrence came about is a grand tale of circumstances, as Jesus had managed to once again escape the long arm of the law in Canada and take refuge with the Lakota people in their beloved Black Hills.

He had been in hiding for several years in a Canadian First Nation's community before receiving what he would term a revelation. He was led to the Black Hills by a voice that was urging him onward in his continuing search for an inkling of justice in a place called America, where justice had gone the way of the dinosaur. It had become extinct, sacrificed at the altar of hypocritical religious arrogance and a devoutly stern commitment to marginalizing the poor while aggrandizing the rich. This was the land where the affluent flaunted their wealth and were coddled by the government while the poor were blamed for being poor. Here, at Pine Ridge, a land of poverty, hopelessness and despair, the people had once been the kings and queens of a mighty empire that embraced compassion and shared the wealth. Their land was stolen. Their way of life trivialized and nearly destroyed. They lived in a cesspool of desperation created by those who saw them as savages clinging to a past that was gone with the wind. However, there was a man walking among them now ready to urge them to get off their knees and not ask for justice but demand it. Yes, Jesus had made his way to the Lakota Nation.

Jesus was not a deliverer of fairy tales. He was a man who told it like it was, and extended the hand of love to encourage all to walk with him in glorious rebellion against the status-quo that had made most people prisoners in a world ruled by and for the 1% at the top of the economic ladder. Jesus was not the savoir of the Bible; he was the modern day Che Guevara leading people from the depth of poverty driven misery courtesy of the privileged class to the heights of the mountaintop that looked down into a tranquil valley where all men were truly equal and free from the tyranny of greed.

<u>PROLOGUE – PART 1</u>
ONE OF HISTORY'S
GREATEST OPPRESSORS

*Many a poet has had his day.
I can remember old Vincent Benoit.
About the Black Hills he had a lot to say.
"I shall not rest quiet in Montparnasse.
I shall not rest easy at Winchelsea.
You may bury my body in Sussexgrass.
You may bury my tongue at Champmedy.
I shall not be there. I shall rise and pass.
For my heart is buried at Wounded Knee."*

To thoroughly understand this incredible story,
one must have some concept of where it takes
place and how the man calling himself Jesus

wound up there. The Pine Ridge Indian Reservation (*Wazí Aháŋhaŋ Oyáŋke* in the Lakota language), and also called the Pine Ridge Indian Agency is a reservation located in the U.S. state of South Dakota. Originally included within the territory of the Great Sioux Reservation, Pine Ridge was established in 1889 in the southwest corner of South Dakota on the Nebraska border. Today it is the eighth-largest reservation in the United States, larger than Delaware and Rhode Island combined.

Among all places in the United States of America, this place is the poorest. Only about 5% of the land is suitable for agriculture. The population of the reservation is around 40,000. Pine Ridge is the site of several events that marked tragic milestones in the history between the Great Sioux Nation and the United States government. Stronghold Table, a mesa in what is today the Oglala-administered portion of Badlands National Park, was the location of the last of the Ghost Dances. The U.S. authorities attempt to repress this movement eventually led to the Wounded Knee Massacre on December 29, 1890. Now, over 125 years later, Jesus had come to the Lakota Nation to do something spectacular that would get these mighty warriors off their knees. He had been called to perform the ghost dance with the spirit of Sitting Bull in order to resurrect the warrior creed and lead the people in an uprising against the U.S. government that had kept them enslaved in poverty on what was more a concentration camp than a reservation. Ignored, denied medical care, stuck in deplorable slum conditions, drinking poisoned water, denied education, rebuked with indifference by a nation that simply could never come to grips with its genocidal past, these humbled people had been reduced to begging for a handout from a hypocritical government that had the gall to declare them ingrates who did not want to get off welfare. When you have been beaten down for so long, you lose the will to fight back. Your spirit is broken, your will to survive tethers on a precipice of despair where one small push sends you tumbling into an abyss of alcoholism, drug addiction and the belief you are subhuman.

Over one hundred and twenty-five years ago, a new religion was born in the heart of a great spiritual leader named Wovoka, renamed Jack Wilson. He told natives that proper practice of a dance he called the ghost dance would reunite the living with spirits of the dead, bring the spirits of the dead to fight on their behalf, make the white colonists leave, and bring peace, prosperity and unity to native peoples throughout the region.

The basis for the Ghost Dance, sometimes called the circle dance, is a traditional form that has been used by many Native Americans since prehistoric times, but this new ceremony was first practiced among Nevada Paiute and the practice soon swept all over the United States, quickly reaching areas of California and Oklahoma. As the Ghost Dance spread from its original source, Native American tribes synthesized selective aspects of the ritual with their own beliefs.

The Ghost Dance was associated with Wilson's (Wovoka's) prophecy of an end to white expansion while preaching goals of clean living, an honest life and cross-cultural tribal cooperation by Native Americans. Practice of the Ghost Dance movement contributed to many Native Americans beginning to fiercely fight against forced assimilation. This refusal led directly to the massacre of 153 innocents by the U.S. Army at Wounded Knee in 1890. It, along with many other similar massacres, is a sorry chapter that substantiates that the greatest genocide in history was not practiced by Hitler but by the U.S. government. Hitler killed six million Jews. It is estimated that the U.S. government was responsible for the *FINAL SOLUTION* of an ethnic group that led to from 15 million to 30 million Native Americans being killed, with some estimates as high as 100 million.

It was falsely rumoured in 1890 that Sitting Bull was practicing the Ghost Dance in the Black Hills after a fearful U.S. government had forbid doing so. Only in the Unites States of America would a government fear a dance.

While being arrested, Sitting Bull, who never actually did the Ghost Dance, was shot. This led to a sense of mounting fear by natives. Chief Spotted Elk, seeking sanctuary at Pine Ridge after fleeing the Standing Rock Agency, where Sitting Bull had been killed, led a band of people to what he hoped would be safety. The families were intercepted by a heavily armed detachment of the Seventh Cavalry, which attacked them, killing many women and children as well as warriors. They cut unborn babies from mother's wombs. They cut off genitals and heads. They paraded skewered body parts around on swords. For their valiant efforts attacking unarmed women, children and old men, they were awarded 20 medals of honour, the most ever awarded in a single engagement. This abomination could have been corrected many times, but Congress refuses to sanction the proof of this massacre by U.S. Army troops.

However, this was not the last shameful detestation at Wounded Knee. A grassroots protest in 1973 escalated into what is referred to as the Wounded Knee Incident. Members of the Oglala Lakota, the American Indian Movement, and other supporters occupied the town in defiance of federal and state law enforcement in an armed protest lasting 71 days. This event inspired

WHEN JESUS CAME TO THE BLACK HILLS
TO DO THE GHOST DANCE
WITH THE SPIRIT OF SITTING BULL

American Indians across the country, but the government, as always, never lived up to promises that were made, and that same government went after leaders of the movement with a vengeance that bordered on the psychotic. One man, Leonard Peltier, has languished in prison for over 40 years as a political prisoner. The government has used him as an example of what happens to those who stand up to authority.

This whole area of America literally flows with the sorrowful, sordid history of a country (the USA) that set out to annihilate an entire race of people it deemed as inferior and standing in the way of progress.

Across the border of South Dakota in Wyoming is the scene of the Native Americans greatest triumph against the American military machine that has subjugated and enslaved millions upon millions all over the world to the culture of greed. It was here, in a beautiful valley in 1876, that the great Lakota Chief Sitting Bull and Chief Crazy Horse combined forces with the Cheyenne and Arapahoe at Little Big Horn to lead a band of warriors against George Armstrong Custer's 7th Cavalry Regiment and killed every soldier.

What appeared to be a glorious victory was actually the last hurrah against an all-powerful military machine in service to mining interests and railroads that had designs on the Black Hills. As always, the U.S. military was an instrument in service to corporations, and Native Americans simply could not be allowed to stand in the way of what was called progress, meaning the pursuit of the almighty dollar.

The late history of the Native Americans is one that tells a sad story of a people deemed inferior by a racist society. They have lived a life of forced incarceration in what the government calls reservations, but are, in fact, nothing more than modern day concentration camps. American hypocrisy never allows for truth. This nation of hypocrites never looks itself in the mirror and sees facts, but rather practices embellishments and justifications for its arrogant disregard of human rights in America and all over the world. There is actually very little freedom for those with no money, and justice is rarely served to the poor. Meanwhile, propaganda fed by corporate media, self-serving government and one particular political party devoted to racist ideology and commitment to an ideal that is nothing but illusion, leads people to embrace religion and guns rather than compassion. Into the cesspool of hypocrisy, now stood a defiant, determined Jesus hoping to rally the Native Americans for one more battle that would lead them to a great victory against one of history's greatest oppressors.

WHEN JESUS CAME TO THE BLACK HILLS
TO DO THE GHOST DANCE
WITH THE SPIRIT OF SITTING BULL

Wounded Knee Massacre (By Oscar Howe)
The U.S. Army in all its Glory

Mass Burial of Native Bodies at Wounded Knee

J. Wayne Frye

**WHEN JESUS CAME TO THE BLACK HILLS
TO DO THE GHOST DANCE
WITH THE SPIRIT OF SITTING BULL**

PROLOGUE - PART 2
YOU AIN'T SEEN NOTHING YET

*I heard it once in a song by Buffy
'Bout racism kinda of stuffy,
Indian legislation is on the desk
Of a do-right Congressman.
Now, he don't know much about the issue,
So he picks up the phone,
And he asks advice of the Senator
Out in Indian country,
A darling of the energy companies,
Which are ripping off what's left of reservations.*

*Learned a safety rule. Don't know who to thank.
Don't stand between the reservation
And the damn corporate bank.*

J. Wayne Frye 21

WHEN JESUS CAME TO THE BLACK HILLS
TO DO THE GHOST DANCE
WITH THE SPIRIT OF SITTING BULL

They'll send in federal tanks.
It isn't nice, but it's reality.
Bury my heart at Wounded Knee deep in the earth.
Cover me with pretty lies.
Bury my heart at Wounded Knee.

They got these energy companies
That want the land,
And they've got churches by the dozen
That offer Jesus' guiding hand,
While leaders sign away Mother Earth
Over to pollution, war and greed.
This is the White Man's evil seed.
Been that way since their birth.
Bury my heart at Wounded Knee deep in the earth.
Cover me with pretty lies.

They get the federal marshals.
They get the covert spies.
They get the liars by the fire,
And Injuns answer to the FBI's.
They lie in court and get nailed,
And men like Peltier go off to jail.
Bury my heart at Wounded Knee.

Transferred in ghostly sequence
To murder and intimidation;
Annie Mae talked about uranium;
Her head was filled with bullets
And her body dumped.
The FBI cut off her hands,

J. Wayne Frye   22

WHEN JESUS CAME TO THE BLACK HILLS
TO DO THE GHOST DANCE
WITH THE SPIRIT OF SITTING BULL

And said she'd died of exposure.
Bury my heart at Wounded Knee deep in the earth.
Cover me with pretty lies.

They had the Gold Rush Wars.
They wanted Injuns to learn to crawl.
Now history gets written in a liars' scrawl.
They tell ya, "Honey, you can still be an Indian
Down at the 'Y' on Saturday nights."
Bury my heart at Wounded Knee deep in the earth.
Cover me with pretty lies.
Bury my heart at Wounded Knee.

Jesus had arrived in the small community of Martin, and local residents and tourists noticed, with some trepidation, this strange looking and thin, bearded man in his thirties, strolling down the streets. He was over six feet tall, with long, scraggily chestnut like hair that flittered about his shoulders with each smooth, long measured stride he took. There was determination in his gait, as if nothing could stand in his way. He wore baggy blue jeans and a loose-fitting white cotton shirt that was obviously about two sizes too big. The shirttail hung out over his pants, going halfway to his knees. His brow was slightly furrowed, his nose prominent and straight, his chin jutted out. Oh, but the feature that stood out above all others was his eyes. Dark, piercing, almost like beacons they twinkled with certain indignation toward what he saw around him.

The glitziness, the garish display of affluence, the self-absorption and the fine automobiles rolling past filled with individuals bedecked in fine clothes and glittering jewels and the indifference they indicated toward the poor who huddled in alleyways on the brisk October morning indicated to this strolling man a society that had no compassion, no heart, no soul. All had been sacrificed at the altar of greed. Greed was the white man's real religion and it had been used to subjugate, humiliate and emasculate. Moving swiftly down the street, all eyes seemed to be following him, as there was something mystically powerful about this simple man.

He moved gracefully down Main Street and made a sudden left turn onto Denver Avenue, walking a few metres until he arrived at a place named Saloon Number 12 on the corner of Williams Street and Denver Avenue. He pushed open the old-time swinging doors and confidently strolled in. The handful of customers all looked up, glaring at what would have been in days past a "damned hippie." A slight grin pursed his lips as he moved to the bar where Harold Pinter, the owner, said, "What the hell are you doing here? I don't believe it. I thought you were dead, killed in the Broughton Archipelago."

WHEN JESUS CAME TO THE BLACK HILLS
TO DO THE GHOST DANCE
WITH THE SPIRIT OF SITTING BULL

A full smile swept slowly across Jesus' lips as his eyes twinkled. "Harold, don't you know I always rise from the dead? You can't keep the son of man dead for long." He then laughed as he continued. "Hey, looks like you were resurrected, too. You have a good thing going here."

Harold bellowed, "Broughton was a very long time ago. I got out with Aaron Adams. He saved my ass, but felt like he had somehow failed, because he didn't save you."

"Aaron! Ah, Aaron Adams, the man of legend he is. Have you heard from him lately?"

"No, he got me through to Port Angeles on the ferry. Handed me some money and told me to disappear until things blew over. Well, they blew over and here I am back among native people. Where else would I feel comfortable? Ah, and you my friend, wherever you are there is soon trouble brewing. Are you here to try to start another revolution?"

"I am here to once again try to get people off their knees, Harold. I know this place is ripe for a revolution of the spirit. For too long, these people have suffered indignity after indignity. I am here, my friend, to do the ghost dance with a very special person. Once again the ghost dance will call people to arms, call them to stand up against the tyranny that has robbed them of their birthright."

"Goddamn, here we go again," said Harold, shaking his head vigorously and shrugging his shoulders. "You have no idea how far down these people have sunk. Getting them off their knees will be a monumental task. Most have simply given up. The last time these people had even a semblance of hope was the 1970's occupation of Wounded Knee. Since then, it has all been down hill, except for this damn pipeline thing."

In order to better understand what follows, it behoves the reader to know some history about the 71 day standoff between Indian activists and the U.S. government at Wounded Knee. Though very brief, it was a time when pride returned to Pine Ridge.

On February 27, 1973, a team of 200 Oglala Lakota (Sioux) activists and members of the American Indian Movement (AIM) seized almost complete control of a town with a loaded history – Wounded Knee, South Dakota. They arrived in town at night in a caravan of cars and trucks, took the town's residents hostage and demanded that the U.S. government make good on treaties from the 19th and early 20th centuries. Within hours, police had surrounded Wounded Knee, forming a cordon to prevent protesters from exiting and sympathizers from entering. This marked the beginning of a 71- day siege and armed conflict.

One of the leaders was a controversial figure named Russell Means, a prominent member of AIM (American Indian Movement). It is not my purpose here as re-teller of this story to judge Russell Means, just suffice it to say that among the Native Americans he had his supporters and his detractors. AIM, itself, was and still is controversial. The Wounded Knee siege was both an inspiration to indigenous people and left-wing activists around the country and, according to the U.S. Marshals Service, which besieged the town along with FBI and National Guard, the longest-lasting civil disorder in 200 years of U.S. history.

Two native activists lost their lives in the conflict, and a federal agent was shot and paralyzed. Like the Black Panthers, AIM was a militant civil rights and identity movement that sprang from the political and social crisis of the 1960s, but it basically passed into obscurity. The Pine Ridge reservation, where Wounded Knee was located, had been in turmoil for years. To many in the area, the siege was no surprise. The Oglala Lakota who lived on the reservation faced racism beyond its boundaries and a poorly managed tribal government within the boundaries. In particular, they sought the removal of tribal chairperson, Dick Wilson, who many Oglala living on the reservation thought corrupt. Oglala Lakota interviewed by PBS for a documentary said Wilson seemed to favour mixed-race, assimilated Lakota like himself, and especially his own family members over reservation residents with more traditional lifestyles. Efforts to remove Wilson by impeaching him had failed, and so Oglala Lakota tribal leaders turned to AIM for help in removing him by force. Their answer was to occupy Wounded Knee. Again, I am not taking sides, just relating facts to help better lay the background for this story.

Federal marshals and National Guard traded heavy fire daily with the native activists. To break the siege, they cut off electricity and water to the town, and attempted to prevent food and ammunition from being passed to the occupiers. (Ironically, none of this was done with the Bundy led siege of a wild life reserve in Oregon in 2016. Of course, they were all white.)

Native Americans were the wrong colour to be given any slack by the federal authorities, so in the Wounded Knee situation a 2,000-pound food drop on the 50th day of the siege was arranged. When the occupiers ran out of the buildings where they had been sheltering to grab the supplies, agents opened fire on them. The first member of the occupation to die, a Cherokee, was hit by a bullet that flew through the wall of a church. So much for the sanctity of a church when occupied by Native Americans.

To many observers, the standoff resembled the Wounded Knee Massacre of 1890 when a detachment of the 7th U.S. cavalry slaughtered a group of Lakota. Suddenly, that same day, the federal agents started pounding the compound with machine gun fire, with tracers flying overhead as if it was a war zone.

With the death of a member, negotiations began in earnest. The militants officially surrendered on May 8, and a number of the AIM members managed to escape the town before being arrested. (Those arrested, including Russell Means, were almost all acquitted because key evidence was mishandled.)

In the three years following the stand-off, Pine Ridge had the highest per capita murder rate in the country. Two FBI agents were among the dead. The Oglala blamed the federal government for failing to remove Wilson as tribal chairperson; the U.S. retorted that it would be illegal for them to do so, somewhat ironically citing reasons of tribal self-determination.

Wounded Knee is actually the Auschwitz of America, only this concentration camp has never ceased to operate. While the USA decries the barbarity of organizations like ISIS and Al Qaeda, the savagery that was practiced by the Nazis and the unbridled support of terrorism by nations it brands as pariahs, it has yet to come to grips with its own terrorism and genocide against natives.

The bartender, Harold Pinter, was visibly concerned about having the man whom he had never accepted as the real Jesus, standing in his bar, attracting attention from the patrons. He whispered, "Damn man, I hope you ain't starting nothing in here. I got a good thing going."

"Start something," replied Jesus. "I start nothing. I just tell people it is time to get off their knees."

"Goddamn it! If you are the person you claim to be, perform a goddamn miracle."

"You want miracles?"

"Yeah, let me see just one miracle. One and I'll believe you are who you say you are and throw my lot in with you. Chuck it all and follow you like your disciples once did."

Jesus, smiling, said, "All my disciples wound up dead. Pretty risky being one of my disciples. You still want miracles?"

"Yeah, one miracle. Come on."

WHEN JESUS CAME TO THE BLACK HILLS
TO DO THE GHOST DANCE
WITH THE SPIRIT OF SITTING BULL

Smiling, Jesus turned to his right and pointed at a burly Native American man in the far corner of the bar leaning against the wall. He was at least 6:4 and had a very muscular build. He turned back to Harold and said, "A real kick-ass I bet?"

"Yep. Don't nobody mess with Peter. He is one damn mean Injun."

"What if I walked over and called him a pussy?"

"Don't do it Jesus. I am warning you. You'll spend the night picking up your teeth off the floor. Anyway, what I the hell does that have to do with a miracle?"

Jesus said, "Watch."

Peter Running Bear was a man who was not necessarily respected but was feared. He had tattoos all over both arms, two lower front teeth missing and projected a fierceness that often made people tremble when he would just give them a look. His powerful fists had dispatched two men to the promised land in a barroom brawl that got him 15 years for manslaughter.

Peter was talking with two white men by the pool table. Jesus walked up, smiled at him, looked back over his left shoulder at Harold and said, "So, this is the guy you say I should fear?"

WHEN JESUS CAME TO THE BLACK HILLS
TO DO THE GHOST DANCE
WITH THE SPIRIT OF SITTING BULL

Shocked, Peter turned and looked down at the 6:1 Jesus and said, "You looking to get your faced flattened asshole?"

Jesus smiled and introduced himself, "Hi, I am Jesus."

All three men laughed uproariously. Peter said, "You mean Hey-Soos. You don't look Mexican, though."

"Nope, I mean Jesus. I'm here to get your people off their knees to demand justice. A pussy like you probably won't follow me though, because you had rather spend time in here shooting pool than shooting at those who keep you in chains. You had rather get drunk than get even."

Harold reached under the bar and fingered the shotgun just in case. He cupped his index finder around the trigger and got ready to pull the gun out. He was breathing heavily as Jesus again looked over his left shoulder and said, "Don't use your gun Harold. You don't need it, because I am going to perform a miracle."

He turned back and stared at Peter. "You want to stay a useless pussy or you want to walk with me into the sunlight of hope and help me lead your people back to their glory days before the white man showed up and stole your birthright?"

WHEN JESUS CAME TO THE BLACK HILLS
TO DO THE GHOST DANCE
WITH THE SPIRIT OF SITTING BULL

Peter's face was flush with anger. He was breathing like a marathoner who had just finished a race. "Who the hell are you?"

"I told you who I was pussy. Now, show me who you are. You a drunken Injun or are you a warrior? Come on, I don't have time to waste. Tell me if you have the nerve to face the hostile army of your oppressors and not flinch. Are you a man who knows that in your body flows the noble blood of a Lakota? Come on! Are you a descendent of men like Sitting Bull and Crazy Horse, or you just a mealy-mouthed pussy who is going to let the white man tell you how useless you are?"

Peter scowled, looked at Jesus with an abiding hatred burned into his eyes and took a long deep breath, tossed the pool cue down on the table and said. "You are a fucking moron if you think I will stand here and not smash your face in and kick your ass out onto the street. No man has ever talked to me this way and not paid a price."

"That is because no man has ever told you the truth about the price of what you are doing. You are playing into the white man's hands. He wants to convince you how worthless you are, and if you are not willing to stand up to his greed, then you are worthless to yourself and to your people. Throw off your chains and walk with me my son, walk with me into trouble like you have never seen before, but it is the kind of trouble that will inspire you."

Peter shook his head fiercely as if he was trying to wake from a dream. A quizzical look slowly spread across his cracked and weathered face. "Your name's Hey-Soos you say?"

"No, absolutely not. I told you my name is Jesus."

The two men standing beside Peter started to move toward Jesus who simply stared at them with his dark penetrating eyes. They froze in their tracks, so intense was his gaze. Jesus stood there for a few seconds before turning to Peter. "So, Peter, what is it to be? You going to keep being a pussy or are you going to remember something I said long, long ago. *Do not think that I came to bring peace on earth. I did not come to bring peace but a sword.*"

Jesus continued, "Walk with me brother and you will be stepping into more trouble than you have ever known in your entire life. I am an unrepentant, wild-eyed, walking, talking revolutionary. I stir up more trouble than a bees' nest that has been disturbed by a honey seeking bear. And believe me, my bite will sting the whole world, especially the world of the privileged and wealthy. I am here to overthrow the rule of the Satan-like U.S. government that stole the sacred Black Hills from you. Walk with me and we shall resurrect the spirit of Sitting Bull and do the ghost dance again, a dance that we will use to trample the United States government and the arrogant bigots who control it under the feet of righteousness that will reverberate all over the world, where so many cry out for justice. Join with me in the dawn of a new day for the Lakota, for the Cheyenne, the Cree, the Arapaho, for all the people who have fallen under the terror of this nation that knows no restraint in its quest to impose the evil of capitalistic corporate greed on the entire world."

Peter smiled, shrugged his enormous shoulders and said, "I may be a damn fool, but there is something about you, something I cannot explain. Let's go."

Peter walked to Jesus and put his right arm around his shoulder. The two of them strolled past the bar where a stunned Harold stood with his hand still on the shotgun. Jesus looked over and smiled as he and Peter headed for the door. "Miracle enough?"

"Not exactly what I had in mind, but calling Peter a pussy and getting away with it is definitely a damn miracle."

WHEN JESUS CAME TO THE BLACK HILLS
TO DO THE GHOST DANCE
WITH THE SPIRIT OF SITTING BULL

Still smiling, when they got to the door, Jesus looked back over his right shoulder and said, "You ain't seen nothing yet."

CHAPTER 1
BLOWING IN THE WIND

*Jesus Christ was the supreme anarchist;
the creative anarchist par excellence,
working not from the top down,
but from the bottom up with the poor
to empower people and enable them
to realize their potential as human beings.*

Mary Morning Dove stood by the banks of the South Fork of the Little White River that was flowing like the grey and silent spectre of her life, swirling about in many tiny whirlpools. She was already starting her early evening drinking, preparing to embrace that which allowed her to cope with a life that had been in a downward spiral since she took her first drink of alcohol at 12. For twenty years, her life as a prostitute made her self-loathing and usually despondent.

Suddenly, a strange feeling overwhelmed her. With arms outstretched toward the heavens, she began a chant. Then, an unusual calm swept over her, calm like she had never felt before. Slowly she turned and there stood her friend Peter Running Bear. Beside Peter was a strange looking, shabbily clothed man. He motioned for her to join him and Peter. He said not a word to her, just beckoned her with a wave of his hand. She slowly, as in a trance, moved toward the two men. Peter said, "We are about to take up the sword against our people's oppressors." They began to walk toward a bright light shining in the distance, as Peter continued. "You won't believe me when I tell you this dude's name, so don't laugh. Just humour him like I am. He goes by the name Jesus."

Mary said, "You gotta be shitting me."

Jesus glanced over at her as they continued walking. "You want to go on drinking your life away, feeling sorry for yourself because you were born into this abysmal poverty that is the result of genocide and unmitigated bigotry, or you want to get off your knees and kick some U.S. government ass?"

WHEN JESUS CAME TO THE BLACK HILLS
TO DO THE GHOST DANCE
WITH THE SPIRIT OF SITTING BULL

She did not look at Jesus, did not answer him. She quizzically said to Peter, "This guy is nuts. What the hell we following him for?"

Shaking his head, Peter replied, "I have no damn idea. All I know is he called me a pussy and the next thing I know here I am following him to God knows where, probably to jail."

Jesus, staring at the immensely bright light far in the distance, said, "Jail is not so bad. In a way, people in jail are a lot freer than those on the outside. For example Peter, you been in jail, and you feel more at home there than on the outside. Am I right?"

"Yes I do. Out here is pure hell sometimes, watching all the greed that makes people walk all over each other. Do anything to get their hands on some damn money. They'll sell their goddamn souls for a few dollars."

Smiling, Jesus said, "You see, it is all a matter of perspective. This nation locks up those who dare question authority. It throws a man who steals a pizza in the slammer, but when a Wall Street tycoon steals billions from people he just declares bankruptcy and is ballyhooed as a smart businessman.

"Goddamn right," interjected Mary.

WHEN JESUS CAME TO THE BLACK HILLS
TO DO THE GHOST DANCE
WITH THE SPIRIT OF SITTING BULL

Jesus said, "You been in jail Mary, many times. Where did you meet the most honest people, out here or inside?"

"Jail!"

"In jail, what you see is what you get. Out here, most people are always acting, always hiding behind a mask. You two come from a noble race of people who had no pretence, but the white man showed up with his Jesus-thing and called the natives heathens. The white man talked about the glory of Jesus and how he was the son-of-God, the pathway to heaven. Only problem with that is they had no idea who the real Jesus was. These hypocrites spoke of love and compassion, but they practiced hatred and arrogance. Nothing has changed in all these years, except that most Native Americans have given up and far too many have embraced the culture of greed, made themselves devotees of the white man's evil.

Peter, empathically said, "You damn right!"

Jesus continued: "It causes consternation and bewilderment. You are trying to fit into a society that is the very opposite of your natural proclivities and inclinations."

As they moved toward the light in the far distance, it began to shimmer. Mary felt great trepidation start to overwhelm her. She reached down and took Peter's hand as she whispered, "What is that light in the distance? It must be at Bear Butte near Wounded Knee?"

Jesus, Peter beside him, tilted his head forward so he could see Mary. "That is the light that will change everything for you. It is going to give you the warmth of my love and the love of your tribal members who are now gathering at a special place in the Black Hills where Sitting Bull is going to do the ghost dance with the son of man. I am called to arouse your people and to guide them out of the darkness that has engulfed them into the bright sunshine of hope that will light a fire that will consume all who dare stand against justice. The God of vengeance from the Old Testament is about to be conjured up. Retribution, Mary Morning Dove, is about to be rendered for all the indignities suffered by native people in this land that has been ruled far too long by the miscreants of mayhem who know absolutely no boundaries to their greed."

Mary and Peter stared at each other as Jesus continued. "Together. We are going to bring down an apocalypse of fury against the evil of greed, bigotry and arrogance."

They were now on the highway, heading toward Bear Butte, where the light was twinkling behind a far hill. A pickup truck was approaching from the rear. It slowed and a man on the passenger side rolled down his window as the truck pulled alongside them. "Going to Sturgis? We'll give you a ride."

Jesus, nodding his head, said, "Yes, we'll take a ride, but we are not going to Sturgis, we are going to glory with Sitting Bull by our side. We'll let you go there with us Philip Big Bear, and your friend doing the driving, Bartholomew Soaring Eagle, can drive us to the bright shining light in the distance that will guide us on our journey to justice."

All were shocked that Jesus knew the names of the two men in the truck. Mary whispered to Peter. "Again, I say to you, who is this dude?"

Philip and Bart stared at one another, and Philip turned to Jesus and said, "How do you know our names? We have never seen you before."

A broad smile crept across Jesus' lips. "The son-of-man knows all names."

Philip, quizzically said, "Who the hell are you?"

"I am Jesus, the man who is going to lead your people in the greatest battle any of the native nations have ever seen. Your defeat of Custer will pale in comparison to what we are about to accomplish. We are going to take on the evil entity that has kept you enslaved far too long. We are going head-to-head with the U.S. government. As the saying goes, "Get ready to rumble!"

Bart, leaning over the steering wheel, shook his head as if he was clearing out the cobwebs of years long past, said, "Hop in the back and when we get to where you are going, give us some of that powerful weed you're smoking. "

Shaking his head, Jesus said, "I am going to give you the most powerful weed imaginable, but it will grow into a beautiful red rose that will glisten with hope, but there will be mighty thorns to prick those who try to snuff out justice. You are about to experience the euphoria of hope. We may not all get there together, because some will have to pay the ultimate price, but all will learn that it is better to die on your feet than live on your knees."

Jesus, Peter and Mary crawled into the truck bed, continuing their journey toward the light in the distance. Bart, almost in a whisper, said to Philip, "Who the fuck is this son-of-a-bitch; you think he escaped from a mental institution?"

Shaking his head, Philip replied, "Don't give a damn. This is a righteous dude. Let's see where this leads. What the hell else do we got to do?"

WHEN JESUS CAME TO THE BLACK HILLS
TO DO THE GHOST DANCE
WITH THE SPIRIT OF SITTING BULL

The radio was tuned to an oldies station and suddenly a prophetic tune sung by the troubadour of lost causes, Bob Dylan, began to play.

How many roads must a man walk down
Before you call him a man?
How many seas must a white dove sail
Before she sleeps in the sand?
And how many times must the cannon balls fly
Before they're forever banned?
The answer, my friend, is blowin' in the wind
The answer is blowin' in the wind

How many years can a mountain exist
Before it's washed to the sea?
How many years can some people exist
Before they're allowed to be free?
How many times can a man turn his head
And pretend that he just doesn't see?
The answer, my friend, is blowin' in the wind
The answer is blowin' in the wind

How many times must a man look up
Before he can see the sky?
How many ears must one man have
Before he can hear people cry?
How many deaths will it take 'till he knows
That too many people have died?
The answer, my friend, is blowin' in the wind
The answer is blowin' in the wind
(Lyrics © BOB DYLAN MUSIC CO.)

CHAPTER 2
ANARCHY GLORIFIED

*Harold Pinter remembered Jesus' friend,
And a frantic message did he send.
Aaron Adams was just relaxing,
But he was about to face something taxing.*

*What did then ensue
Received a scribe's due.
Aaron had been by Jesus' side,
And twice watched as hope died.*

*Shaking his head in bewilderment and frustration,
He knew he had to go to the Lakota Nation.
Why would not Jesus let sleeping dogs lie?
"OK, here we go again," Aaron did sigh.*

WHEN JESUS CAME TO THE BLACK HILLS
TO DO THE GHOST DANCE
WITH THE SPIRIT OF SITTING BULL

Aaron Adams answered the phone and a frantic Harold Pinter said, "Aaron, he is back?"

Aaron immediately knew who was on the phone and that Harold was talking about Jesus. He had once saved Jesus from certain death by putting him on a train in New Jersey bound for Canada. Then, he had seen him crucified and assumed him dead on a small Canadian island. Shaking his head, because he knew that trouble and Jesus were synonymous, he asked Harold, "What the hell is he doing in the Black Hills? No, you don't have to tell me. What else but stirring up trouble."

"Are you coming," pleaded Harold.

Sighing, Aaron replied, "Hell, I shouldn't, but what can I do? The guy walks around thinking he is Jesus, and frankly I ain't so sure he isn't. Damn, he is a frustrating bastard. O.K., I am on my way. Will be there in a few hours."

"Thanks Aaron. He wouldn't listen to me."

"And you think he'll listen to me?"

While Aaron was winging his way on a chartered plane to the Deadwood Airport, Jesus and his retinue were moving steadily toward that bright light in the distance. As they passed a large contingent of natives by the side of the road, Jesus pounded on the back window and signaled Philip to stop. The cadre of walkers sauntered up by the truck and Jesus said, "Welcome my friends. Climb in Andrew, John and you two men called James." Looking at the two men named James; one had long, flowing white hair, so Jesus said to him. "I shall call you James the Elder and your younger friend I shall call James the Younger."

Mystified at how this stranger knew their names, they crawled into the back of the truck as Peter said, "Don't ask any questions. Nothing makes sense with this dude but for some reason me, Mary, Bart and Philip are along for the ride."

As they turned a curve at the top of a hill, the headlights cast an eerie glow on the mesa to their right at the bottom of which a group of men were huddled around a barrel with a roaring fire. They were passing around a bottle. Jesus again tapped on the back window, indicating the truck should stop. The men knew all in the truck but Jesus and waved them over to share their libations. Jesus said, "Come on a journey. Put down that false elixir of hope and join me. I shall give you the elixir of life." He then pointed at the flickering light in the far distance and continued. "That is the light of life - a better life for you and your people. Thaddeus, Matthew, Simon and Thomas – take a chance. You have nothing to lose but your chains." He then pointed over at a lone figure leaning against a rock, seemingly in deep thought. "And you Iudas, come and arrest the doubts of your purpose in life. You are about to end a lifetime of searching for meaning. Come all of you and grasp a bottle that is filled with hope and direction. Come with me, as I am going to Bear Butte or as you call it, Mathó Pahá, where Crazy Horse received his greatest vision, and there awaits the spirit of Sitting Bull. We shall do the ghost dance and the great Lakota Nation shall rise up in unison and throw its shackles into the Badlands of the Dakotas to trample them under warriors feet as a great uprising is about to occur. Come, hop onto this truck which is the vehicle that takes the son-of-man to his destiny."

Thomas, the one with the most doubt, stood silently while the others piled on board. Iudas was by Thomas' side. They stared at Jesus as he said, "You doubt Thomas. That is good, and there by your side Iudas admires your doubting, as do I. Never take anything at face value. You see me as a brownish man with a flowing long shirt and a craggily beard. Who am I to follow? I tell you who I am. I am the man who is going to reach the inner heart of your people and rekindle their pride."

Thomas looked at Iudas, who stood in total bewilderment and said, "Get on board. We'll give this man a chance to prove he is worthy of our devotion and respect." Jesus then extended his hand and helped pull Thomas onto the truck bed. Thus did 14 people fill that little truck, as it rambled toward Bear Butte (Mathó Pahá) and a rendezvous with destiny.

Thomas was inquisitive and asked his name. When Jesus told him, Thomas said, "You mean Hey-soos?"

Peter did not give Jesus a chance to answer. "No, he means Jesus."

Thomas had a quizzical look on his face as Jesus said, "Does it matter my name? I am a simple man with a message of love, but love is not always the answer when seeking justice. You must be forceful in demanding justice."

"Are you saying that violence is the answer to our problems?" asked Andrew.

"I am saying that when you have begged, when you have pleaded, when you have been trampled by indifference that sometimes the only answer understood by those with their boot on your neck is violence. If a man is choking the life out of you, you can plead for mercy, but if it is not forthcoming, you must defend yourself with all the strength you can muster. Have not the people here pleaded long enough? Are they to continue supplicating themselves before the jacked-booted cretins of greed who know no end to their desire for more and more?"

Puzzled, Andrew said, "We have lost our way it is true, but if the people have bread on the table, they are willing to bow before the white man. We have lost the will to fight."

Jesus, eyes fiery with determination, replied, "Ah, but is it not said that man does not live by bread alone. Do we all not need greater sustenance than the food that fills our bellies? I once was in the desert for 40 days and though my belly was empty, my soul was filled. That was the nourishment that guided me into the arms of a good Samaritan who through benevolence eased my thirst and vanquished my hunger. Does not the Lakota Nation need to vanquish its hunger?"

Thaddeus said, "You sound like a Bible-thumping Christian. We've had enough of them."

"I do not call myself a Christian, for that is a word that carries a sad connotation, because it has been perverted in its meaning. Christians have always been taught to judge and condemn, not embrace and accept. There is a wise saying which urges man not to see the sawdust in his brother's eye while paying no attention to the plank in his own eye?"

WHEN JESUS CAME TO THE BLACK HILLS
TO DO THE GHOST DANCE
WITH THE SPIRIT OF SITTING BULL

All in the truck bed were amazed at the depth to this incredible man's profound words. Peter said, "We are all stuck in such misery here. We have lost all hope."

"The people who live in darkness will see a great light," he said as he pointed to the beam of light drawing ever nearer now. "Look behind us, can you not see the row of lights following us toward the light. All over, by car, by truck, by horse, by motorcycle, by bicycle, people are converging on Bear Butte, called by the desire to be led from the darkness into the light. All of you are here, because you are going to stand by my side as we lift your people up from the depths of despair and give them hope. We, my dear friends, are about to perform a miracle that will resurrect the warrior spirit and this great nation will once again tread the scared Black Hills with a swagger of confidence and the spirit of warriors."

Aaron squirmed on the plane. Looking out into the darkness, he contemplated how, in the past, this man calling himself Jesus had miraculously appeared out of nowhere in a small New Jersey town and caused such a commotion that the church and government feared his message. The two colluded to eliminate him and keep the people from seeing he was offering hope to end oppression by the wealthy and privileged. He helped him escape. Then, several years later, Jesus popped up on a sparsely populated island trying to lead an indigenous rebellion. The results were disastrous, as Aaron assumed his friend was brutally killed by U.S. Special Forces sent in to force the American will upon those who dared stand against tyranny. Aaron whispered to himself, "He has risen, been resurrected to once again walk in defiance of the abominations of militarism, poverty and greed?" He laughed quietly to himself, shaking his head that he would even countenance the idea of a deity.

Suddenly, as he peered over the wing, watching a slow stream of exhaust from the engine, he closed his eyes and began to see a series of visions dancing in his head.

As he lay asleep in the airplane,
There came a voice from a raging sea,
And with great power it forth led him
To walk in the visions of all he could see.

He met murder on his way.
Murder had very little to say.
Very smooth, but he was grim.
A dark cloud hung over him.

There were seven civil servants following.
My, it was human hearts they were swallowing.
Tossed by murder for them to chew,
Which from his black cloak he drew.

WHEN JESUS CAME TO THE BLACK HILLS
TO DO THE GHOST DANCE
WITH THE SPIRIT OF SITTING BULL

One of the followers was slowly moving on.
You knew there was something terribly wrong.
Big tears of wailing he wept falsely well,
Turning to stones as on the ground they fell.

And the little native children, who
Round his feet played, knew no foe.
They were thinking every tear a gem,
But had their brains knocked out by him.

One other servant was clothed in light,
But his eyes were dark and evil as night.
On his brow hypocrisy did laughingly lie,
As it was the result of America's deathly sigh.

Many, many more destructions played
In this ghastly arrogant masquerade,
Righteousness disguised, even to the eyes,
As natives fell before white men's lies.

Last came anarchy; and he rode
On a gallant horse, hope to sow.
He was pale even to the lips,
Like Death in the Apocalypse.

And he wore the kingly crown,
For in his word greatness was found.
And he had the mark of mayhem
That sparkled all about him.

With a pace stately and fast,

J. Wayne Frye　　　　53

WHEN JESUS CAME TO THE BLACK HILLS
TO DO THE GHOST DANCE
WITH THE SPIRIT OF SITTING BULL

Over heartbroken land he passed.
Trampling politicians in his wake,
He shouted "This is for your sake."

A mighty troop of the indignant formed around,
Shouting for justice, trampling shook the ground.
Waving each a bloody lance,
They vowed to give anarchy a chance.

Aaron awoke, blinking his eyes as he could faintly make out the Black Hills below in the darkness. Had he really been dreaming or had he had a vision. This was the land of visions: Crazy Horse, Black Elk, Sitting Bull had all received great visions in this mystic land. And, what of the great vision by the originator of the ghost dance, Wovoka, who saw the re-emergence of the Indian nations and the dawning of a new day when the tribes would all find their former glory and the white man would be defeated and the sacred Black Hills protected against exploitation?

Ah, but the Jesus that Aaron had known came not to bring peace but a sword. He was a fiery revolutionary, not a meek man who turned the other cheek. Anarchy followed him like a shadow. Yes, anarchy! Was Jesus about to rain down anarchy in the name of justice?

Aaron could see a bright light far in the distance near a butte far to the left of the plane. While he was anxiously anticipating seeing his old friend, Jesus was among the native people, about to stir up passion with his fiery rhetoric.

As the motley crew piled out of the truck, all around them were masses of Lakota men, women and children. They had all been curious about the light, but many had come from a great distance just because of an inner voice that urged them to be at Bear Butte. There must have been at least 3000 people there, all anticipating some great occurrence. An intense silence fell among the crowd as Jesus, followed by his 13 friends made his way toward a large rock in the distance. This man of great wisdom walked boldly through the crowd, as it grew ever larger.

How does one adequately describe the power emanating from this slight figure of a man? He was somewhat tall, and comely, with a very reverent countenance, such as beholders might both love and fear him. His long, flowing chestnut hair, full but still very scraggily, hung over his ears, whence downwards it was curlier and wavering about his shoulders. In the midst of his head was a centre part. His forehead was plain and very delicate, his face without a spot or a wrinkle, seeming to have a glow about it. His nose was a bit large and the mouth had an irreverent twist. His beard thick and scraggily, in colour like his hair, was not very long. His look was innocent and mature. His eyes were dark and intense, and so clear one could see deep within them into the soul of a great man. Anyone smitten with hypocrisy could see an instant rebuke in his twinkling eyes. He moved among the hushed crowd courteous and fair in his manner, often touching the heads of little children. He made short pleasant remarks to a few. There was gravity in his manner, almost as if he was weeping for those among him. There was determination though in each stride. He seemed to relish reaching out with his hands to touch those there, and when he did render touch there was a surge of love that seemed to flow from him to those present.

Peter helped him up onto the rock that led to a cave opening behind him. The crowd was becoming anxious, wondering why the light now shining brightly in the cave behind Jesus had suddenly, a few hours before, seemingly summoned them all to the butte. Jesus waved his right hand and an instant hush fell upon the crowd. All stood in complete silence, even the small children, anticipating the words from him.

"You have all been summoned here tonight by a force that you cannot explain, and it is you who will spread the word to all the Lakota that your deliverance is at hand." He turned and looked back at the cave where the light was growing brighter. "Tonight I have come to do the ghost dance with the spirit of Sitting Bull. I am a man who loves peace, but often the peace lovers are perceived as weak. All of you must look into your hearts and ask yourself if peace will get you justice from those in Washington who have trampled on your rights with impunity for hundreds of years. Look about the place you call home. There is poverty in the midst of plenty, because you have all bowed before the tyranny of a government that stole your birthright. The greed that feeds those in the seats of power has devoured your hopes, dreams and aspirations. They disrespect your religion while they shove their religion down your throats. They call you heathens while they promote a fairy tale about a saviour who died for your sins. What sins have you committed? Did you take land for gold? Did you turn your backs on your fellow humans in the name of greed? Did you commit genocide against a noble race of people? Did you wall off those who were not white in concentration camps of despair? Did you sign treaty after treaty promising justice and then ignore them before the ink was dry on the paper? Did you take children away from their parents and force them to worship an alien God?"

The throng was captivated, enthralled, mesmerized with each single word that so elegantly flowed from his lips. "I am called Jesus. It is a name you know well I am sure. A name often used to imprison people rather than free them. The church has made an abomination of what that name represents. It has embraced greed as if sanctioned by God. Believe me; if there is a God, he has no room in his heart for greed. To you I say that my name henceforth shall be synonymous with anarchy! The Lakota Nation is about to rise up in unison and rain down upon the oppressors righteous indignation. We shall offer peace, but if it is not accepted, then the fires of hell shall rise up from the bowels of the earth and devour all that stands between us and justice."

A wave of euphoric pride and determination swept through the crowd like an ancient plague. It was as if years of frustration were miraculously stayed by the power of one man's words. An airplane could be seen circling to land in the far distance. Jesus let a slow, methodical smile creep across his lips as he said, "A man named Aaron Adams is on his way to the reservation. He shall join us in this fight. Remember that name, because he is my strong right arm, a man who will help us in the coming struggle. He is blessed in spirit. And you my poor brethren are also blessed in spirit. Put aside that other spirit you find in a bottle and cast it away as you embrace hope."

He glanced back over his shoulder, as the light was now growing less intense. "You are like me, poor in material wealth, but you are blessed with love for one another and for your people. I have sensed your mourning for a life stolen, and I am here to comfort you. You have all been meek, and I once said that the meek will inherit the earth, but I tell you today that being meek before injustice only gets you more injustice. You all long for the righteousness of hope and that shall be fulfilled. You were once told that the merciful shall obtain mercy, but look at the government, look at the corporations, look at the wealthy, look at all your oppressors and ask yourself if they will ever give you mercy. You live in a nation where the poor are blamed for being poor, but I tell you the blame lies with a system that aggrandizes greed as an enviable trait. That system is an abomination. This is a system that laughs in the face of peacemakers. We are anarchists and we shall say woe to the rich, woe to those who see hunger and turn their backs, woe to those who carry a Bible in one hand and bombs and bullets in the other, woe to the hypocrites who profess love while never practicing it. Strive for peace, but prepare for war. Become militants and assemble your weapons. Be not afraid, for weapons in the hands of those abused by an inequitable system of greed are righteous instruments of anarchy. Those who have been trampled on shall now all begin to rise up like mighty lions from slumber."

Someone in the crowd shouted, "Are you God, oh exalted one?"

WHEN JESUS CAME TO THE BLACK HILLS
TO DO THE GHOST DANCE
WITH THE SPIRIT OF SITTING BULL

Smiling, Jesus said, "I tell you with pride that I am anarchy. Embrace me for salvation and deliverance."

Jesus turned and began to walk toward the cave opening. All there were aghast, captivated at what they saw. Within the undulating light, a figure wearing a chief's war bonnet could be faintly made out in the form of an outline, a darkness within the light. The people all began to form a circle and a few brought out eagle feathers, and held them up toward the starlit sky. As Jesus moved into the light, he was embraced by the outline of the man in the war bonnet. While Jesus and the figure embraced, they began to dance in a circle and sing in cadence.

Among the crowd, lines were formed, with one person standing directly behind another, each with his hands on his neighbour's shoulders. After weaving about a few times, chanting, "Father, we come," they set up the most fearful, heart-piercing wails, moaning, groaning and shrieking out their grief that had been held in for so many years. They began naming their departed friends and relatives, and at the same time taking up handfuls of dust at their feet, washing their hands in it, and throwing it over their heads. Finally, they raised their eyes to heaven, their hands clasped high above their heads and stood straight and perfectly still, invoking the power of the Great Spirit to allow them to see and talk with their people who had died. It was then that Jesus stepped aside from his ghost dance with the man in the war bonnet. This man gradually moved from the light away from Jesus where he stood for all to see. The shouts reverberated off the mesa "Sitting Bull, Sitting Bull, Sitting Bull!"

All there began to undulate, shake and shout, their hands moving from side to side, their bodies swaying, their arms, with hands gripped tightly in their neighbours', swinging back and forth with all their might. If one, more weak and frail, came near falling, he or she would be jerked up and into position until tired nature gave way. The ground was worked and worn by many feet, until the fine, flour-like dust lay light and loose to the depth of several centremetres. The wind, which had increased, would sometimes take it up, enveloping the dancers and hiding them from view. In the ring were men, women and children; the strong and the robust, the weak, the consumptive, and those near to death's door. They chanted "Father, I come; Mother, I come; Brother, I come; Great Spirit, give us back our arrows of righteousness."

Jesus moved beside the spirit of Sitting Bull. Many fell to the ground with every muscle twitching and quivering. They seemed to be unconscious. Some of the men and a few of the women would run, stepping high and pawing the air in a frightful manner. Then, with a wave of the hand, Jesus signalled for silence among the throng there as the spirit of Sitting Bull made its way back to the cave as other dark figures stood in the entrance.

Some in the crowd said that it was not Sitting Bull, but merely someone dressed as him, and that the lights were just an elaborate hoax. Jesus had an answer to those doubters. "I claim no supernatural powers. I do not claim to be the son of God, because you are all the sons and daughters of God. What you have seen cannot be explained rationally, but we do not need to be rational. Maybe I have mass hypnotized you all. What difference does it make whether the spirit of Sitting Bull is here or not? He is in each one of you. His spirit lives, if you call upon and honour it. I am here to tell you that if you depend on the supernatural that you have no hope for redemption of this nation, but if you rely on yourselves, rely on your own courage, then there is a way out of your misery. Go and tell others of what you have experienced here and prepare yourselves for battle. It is time to once again put on your war paint and face your oppressor. I shall, in the days ahead, be among you, helping spread the word of the new day. We must arouse the great Lakota spirit. It will sweep over the Black Hills and the people shall know hope and courage again. Fear not death, fear life that is like death."

WHEN JESUS CAME TO THE BLACK HILLS
TO DO THE GHOST DANCE
WITH THE SPIRIT OF SITTING BULL

As the other dark outlines of light faded into oblivion, one tall, faint, muscular figure with a prominent nose stood to Sitting Bull's left. The great chief reached down with his left hand and lifted the other man's right hand as they stood there side-by-side. Suddenly whispers could be heard in the crowd, voices gradually rising until someone shouted, "Crazy Horse! The spirit of Crazy Horse stands with Sitting Bull."

Shaking their clasped hands high above their heads, the two figures, turned and proceeded into the light behind them and the cave slowly went dark as they disappeared. As the crowd was standing in complete awe, Jesus said, "Beware of false prophets, which come to you in sheep's clothing, but inwardly are ravening wolves. You shall know them by their fruits. Do men gather grapes of thorns, or figs of thistles? Even so, every good tree brings forth good fruit, but a corrupt tree brings forth evil fruit. Every tree that brings not forth good fruit is only fit to be hewn down and cast into the fire. Wherefore by their fruits you shall know the good from the evil. Sitting Bull and Crazy Horse saw evil in Custer, and they culled that tree. I say unto you, the U.S. government is an evil tree with bitter fruit. Although a few branches may bear sweet fruit, the tree itself is corrupt and that corruptness is growing stronger, as the branches of bitterness overshadow those of sweetness. Get your axes and we shall cut that tree of unmitigated evil and the sacred Black Hills shall become the Garden of Eden, where strong trees bearing sweet fruit shall sprang to life and nourish the people."

"Therefore, take up the whole armour of righteousness for the Lakota people that you may be able to withstand the evil this nation will put before you. America's array of powerful weapons meant to intimate the entire world and instil fear in all that dare challenge it will make the Black Hills rumble with their war machine. However, we have the spirit of the Lakota people, the spirit of Sitting Bull, Crazy Horse, Gall, Two Moons and all the other great leaders who know that the sacredness of the Black Hills must be protected from the culture of greed that destroys everything in its path. We serve a noble cause to protect the mother earth, not defile it as those who bow before greed do. We shall not waver before any army, for we are an army of righteousness that will slay all who dare dishonour the sacred Black Hills."

He paced about in silence for a few seconds, seemingly in deep, contemplative thought and then continued. "We do not just wrestle against flesh and blood, for flesh and blood is easily defeated. We are wrestling against the evil of freshly minted rulers of this land, put there by those who in their bigotry and ignorance backed an abomination, a man with no moral core, a man who was handed everything he has on a silver platter. He is the epitome of the evil represented by greed. He is the poster child for the indulgent, selfish, insatiable, avaricious desire to possess more and more."

Jesus waved his right hand across his chest and said with determination, "Go forth and gather your weapons. This nation honours the gun more than it honours justice. Before long, those who worship the Second Amendment shall rue the day that they refused to exercise some sanity in gun control. They have made it possible to put weapons in Native American hands with no restraints. The white man is about to reap what he has sown. They have planted the wind and shall reap the whirlwind. The waving grain on the stalks has no head; it shall yield no flour, for these evil men have turned their backs on justice. Prepare my brethren."

He motioned for all those with whom he had shared the truck ride to join him high on the rock so all there could see them. These common men, who were suddenly feeling a surge of pride and hope, leaped upon the rock. Mary though did not move, so Jesus looked at her, smiled and said, "Are you not one of us? Come, join with those who may become martyrs in a grand cause. We may all die, but we will die as one, devoted to a noble endeavour."

WHEN JESUS CAME TO THE BLACK HILLS
TO DO THE GHOST DANCE
WITH THE SPIRIT OF SITTING BULL

He pointed at the 13 he had picked and said, "These are my disciples. They are here to help lead you out of bondage. Heed their advice for they are my favoured ones. They are anarchy glorified!"

CHAPTER 3
YOU ARE ALREADY DEAD

*And with glorious triumph, they
Rode letting deeds hypocrisy slay.
Justice was their intoxication.
Anarchy had great determination.*

*O'er fields and towns, from sea to sea,
Passed the pageant swift and free,
Tearing up, and trampling down,
Till they came to Washington town.*

*And each politician panic-stricken,
Felt their hearts with terror sicken,
Hearing the tempestuous cry
"Anarchy, anarchy, you shall all die!"*

J. Wayne Frye   67

WHEN JESUS CAME TO THE BLACK HILLS
TO DO THE GHOST DANCE
WITH THE SPIRIT OF SITTING BULL

For with prompt determination, Anarchy came,
Clothed in arms like blood and flame.
No more hired murderers did sing,
Anarchy was God and Law and King.

Natives had waited, weak and alone,
For Anarchy the reservations to comb.
Their purses empty, as whites had left them cold,
Now Anarchy offered psychological gold.

All those whom Jesus had picked up to serve by his side marvelled at their newfound confidence and pride. Something had changed inside them.

"Go forth my friends; spread the word that the Lakota Nation must arm itself, put on war paint and prepare for Armageddon if necessary, because no more shall this nation bow before tyranny. I say again that you do not get justice by begging for it. You get justice by demanding it."

As the throng, filled with pride and determination dissipated into the night, Jesus and his disciples crawled into the truck and Jesus said, "To the Number 12 Salon."

Philip said, "We having drinks?"

Jesus replied, "No, there shall be no more drinks. You have all tipped the bottle enough and swallowed the white man's brew of deceit that has captured your souls, put you in concentration camps of despair and stolen your birthright. It is time for you to get intoxicated on the pursuit of justice. Follow me and I promise you nothing but trouble as you rise from slumber and roar like mighty lions while learning what it is like to be alive, really alive. So, we now go to Number 12 Salon and we shall meet a man of character, integrity and devotion to justice, a man who has stood by me twice before in battle."

Aaron Adams, having driven two hours from Deadwood, was standing at the bar talking to Harold as Jesus walked in with his followers. "My friend Aaron Adams, what took you so long?"

Aaron moved toward Jesus and they fondly embraced. "Took me so long? I was here faster than a Republican promising to cut taxes."

Laughing, Jesus introduced all those with him to Aaron, and after introducing Mary, he paused and said, "This is the man who finds me frustrating and demanding, but he knows that in my heart beats a desire for justice, so he stands by me with grand fervour, because he, too, is a man who never accepts injustice without a fight. He has no religion and laughs at those who believe in that thick black book that he looks on as nothing but fairy tales. He thinks Jesus is nothing but a myth. Still, he cannot figure me out. He has doubts, but never has any doubts about standing against injustice."

Shaking his head, Aaron said, "If you are who you say you are, let's see a miracle. How about getting that fine looking young girl over there to come over and offer an old man a romp in paradise."

"Hey, resurrecting the dead is no problem. Giving the blind sight is a breeze. Making the lame's legs straighten and having them do an Irish jig is child's play, but getting a young, good-looking woman interested in a limp-dicked, shrivelled-up old man is way out of my league. That is beyond miracles."

"Still a goddamn smart-ass I see," offered Aaron.

Slapping Aaron on the back, as he leaned onto the bar and winked at Harold, Jesus said, "I have a big job for you. I am here to lead these people in a battle that will make Little Big Horn pale in comparison. I need a strong right arm to ferret out some information as we prepare to take on the biggest terrorist outfit in the world."

"Goddamn, you are going up against the United States government. Aren't two loses to them enough?"

WHEN JESUS CAME TO THE BLACK HILLS
TO DO THE GHOST DANCE
WITH THE SPIRIT OF SITTING BULL

"When you lose, you learn. I have learned a lot, and I am about to put it to use. I just regret that buffoon George Bush is no longer President. Bringing that arrogant rich boy down would be a lot of fun, but the current buffoon will do."

"What the hell are you going to do now? Moreover, I know that damn light I saw from the plane had something to do with you. Tell me how much trouble I'm going to get in this time."

Mary, finding Aaron, despite his 65 years, an appealing man, said, "He has just done the ghost dance with the spirit of Sitting Bull."

"Yeah, and I just got the goddamn fucking Christian fundamentalists to vote for Democrats. Bullshit."

All there had a good laugh, but Jesus abruptly said, "Whether I danced with the spirit of Sitting Bull or not is immaterial. Hey, it might have just been a hallucination, or maybe mass hypnotism. The point is that these people needed a vision and I gave them one."

Peter said, "What do we do next?"

"When is the next tribal council meeting?"

"It is tomorrow," replied Mary.

WHEN JESUS CAME TO THE BLACK HILLS
TO DO THE GHOST DANCE
WITH THE SPIRIT OF SITTING BULL

"Then get a good night's rest and we will go to this meeting, and make sure as many people as possible are there, because we are about to raise hell at Pine Ridge," replied Jesus as he slapped Aaron on the back and continued. "You my friend shall get us a room for the night, because, as usual, I have no funds."

Shrugging his shoulders, Aaron replied, "Of course, what's new?"

As they sat in the room, watching CNN, Jesus was in deep thought as news of a demonstration against the new billionaire President was being analyzed as an exercise in futility, because all branches of the government were firmly in control of white right wing Christian capitalists who were handing the country over to the rich and privileged with no regard for the middle class and poor. The war against the middle class and poor started by President Reagan was finally drawing to a close, and the triumph of the 1% was almost complete. Jesus turned to Aaron and said, "They think they have finally won because they fooled the angry old white men and a few of the white women into voting against their self-interest, and the populace will simply, as they always do, accept their fate with nothing more than whimpers. However, I tell you that the people of the Black Hills shall not go into the gentle night with a whimper. They, my friend, will rage like lions against the storm of hypocrisy. There is a mighty tempest brewing in these hills, and years of frustration are about to be unleashed in a torrent of terror upon all who dare stand against justice for these noble people."

"My friend, you have riled people up before and look what came of it. The last time the American military machine nearly wiped out an entire island. I saw you crucified in the Broughton Archipelago, and I have no idea how you did not die, but this time, you will die. I can assure you that messing with the American government is the height of lunacy. I saw you hanging on a cross after the general ordered his troops to crucify you and let you act like Jesus since you thought you were the Christ. By the way, just how the hell did you survive. When I left, I saw you hanging there, not breathing."

Smiling broadly, Jesus replied, "Why Aaron, do you not know that the son of man died, was buried and rose on the third day?"

Shaking his head, Aaron got up, turned and looked back at Jesus. "Fuck you. I'm going to bed."

As Aaron lay in bed, staring at the ceiling, his brain cleared and there swept back across the threshold of his memory the vivid picture of the horrors he had endured with Jesus in New Jersey and the Broughton Archipelago. He could hear the awful moans and frantic cries of a group of Canadian First Nations people falling under the brutal assault by the U.S. military. Since his service in Vietnam, he had suffered the depression of a man who had fought on the wrong side, the side that represented the evil of exploitation and greed. That war was just another in the long line of wars since the Korean War that was promulgated by a nation that was determined to put all humanity under the terror of capitalistic exploitation. The insidious spread of the evil of American greed was fanning out unimpeded across the world, save a few places that managed to protect the poor and the middle class from complete domination by the 1%. Evil was afoot everywhere, and it was not the Muslims, but the American corporate military machine that was enslaving humanity. Muslims were only a minor irritant used to scare the masses, while the real evil of privilege marched unimpeded to enslave more and more in the eternal pursuit of profit at the expense of humanity.

The next morning Jesus went with Aaron to the Sojourn Café for breakfast. A family of Native Americans came in, and sat at the table beside them. The mother and father were probably in their early forties, and the three children were teenagers. They kept staring at Jesus, until one child said, "You were at Bear Butte last night."

"I was indeed."

"Are you Wovoka?

"No, I am Jesus, and I am here to lead your nation in a battle against the evil of the white devils of commerce who have no respect for your sacred land. We shall destroy their pipeline. We shall destroy their land grabs that trample on your sacred grounds. We shall stand in defiance against the evil that makes slaves of all but the few. Your mother and father there can teach you to be warriors, or teach you to be complacent wimps who accept slavery without a fight." He then stood up, and before all there said, "And you white people may also join the fight. We welcome those who stand with justice and against the evil that has made these noble people slaves in their own land. Come to the council meeting tonight and stand with me and all who fight against injustice. The NRA wants everyone to have a gun, but they are about to shake and tremble in fear once the riled-up Native Americans all have guns to defend their land."

Aaron very quickly got up and grabbed Jesus by the arm as a few white men starting moving his way. One white man shouted, "Out, out you rebel rousing asshole. This is no place to rile people up. We don't need no long-haired hippie commie bastard causing trouble around here."

WHEN JESUS CAME TO THE BLACK HILLS
TO DO THE GHOST DANCE
WITH THE SPIRIT OF SITTING BULL

As three other white men approached in obvious anger, Jesus stood there, without hesitation and a slow methodical smile creased his lips. "Ah, you want to join the fight against tyranny?"

One of the three, a man of maybe 40, who was tall with broad shoulders and massive arms filled with tattoos, replied, "No, we are here to kick your ass."

Jesus, still smiling broadly and showing absolutely no fear, in a calm, measured tone, said, "My, aren't we nasty today," as he looked into his eyes. Aaron started to move between the two, but Jesus said, "No Aaron, this is a man who has been brought up in ignorance. I am about to educate him."

The man shouted, "You goddamn asshole. I ain't ignorant, and I ain't about to let some hippie looking freak scare me."

"Not ignorant uh? You are a poster-boy for ignorance. I bet you vote for guns and against welfare queens every election, but I bet you have no idea that you are also voting against your self-interests. I bet you fall for the garbage spewed out by politicians saying that the poor on welfare are robbing you blind, but you are too stupid to see that the real welfare queens and kings are the rich who are playing you for a sucker."

WHEN JESUS CAME TO THE BLACK HILLS
TO DO THE GHOST DANCE
WITH THE SPIRIT OF SITTING BULL

The three men were now seething with anger, but the stare from Jesus was so intense that they froze in their tracks. Not missing a beat, Jesus continued, addressing the whole restaurant, not just the three men. "You are all slaves to the 1%, but you have all been played by a system that tells you," and then he pointed at the native family, "that these people are the cause of all your troubles. It is not the poor who are stealing from you but the rich. You people are pitiful, and I should not even bother with you, but I am the son of man, and I am here to tell you that as long as you turn your minds over to manipulation, you shall always be in bondage. I am telling you that you can do one of three things. You can help lead in this fight against the forces of evil, you can follow me into battle, or you can get out of the way, because nothing will stop the march toward justice."

The entire room was in awe of the boldness from this seemingly meek man. Jesus smiled broadly, as the three dumbfounded men stood staring in disbelief. Then he looked at the native kids sitting at the table, winked at them and turned to Aaron. "Come on kemosahbee."

As they walked out, Aaron whispered, "Most of these people are too young to have ever seen the *Lone Ranger*. They have no idea what kemosahbee means."

"Ah, but the one whom I want to impress does know what it means."

"It means faithful friend," said Aaron, shaking his head as they walked down the street. "But being your faithful friend comes with a lot of disadvantages and a very high price."

Jesus laughed. "Come on kemosahbee?"

Aaron, noticing a crowd now forming behind them, all natives except for a few whites, said, "I see you are about to give one of your incendiary speeches. No doubt, you are going to lead them into the park, and there you will spellbind them with oratory. I am earnestly warning you that you are playing with fire here. You realize the FBI has jurisdiction on reservations. Messing with the local constabulary is one thing, but messing with the FBI is not healthy in nation that will not tolerate dissent. You know what they did to Leonard Peltier. This is Pine Ridge, and believe me, when wind of what you are advocating gets back to Washington, there will be a bevy of law enforcement officers descending on this place."

The crowd following them was steadily growing. Jesus was heading toward Two Moccasins Park. He was picking up his stride now, as the adrenalin was pumping with a fury though his veins. How he loved to stir up people.

WHEN JESUS CAME TO THE BLACK HILLS
TO DO THE GHOST DANCE
WITH THE SPIRIT OF SITTING BULL

As they entered the park, Aaron was now pleading with him. "Why the hell do you expect me to be involved with your fucking revolutionary incitement that only leads to lost hope? Give up. You are never going to change the complacency of people. Don't you realize that people in this country have given up? Just look at the person they have as President. The white man is back in control, and he is going to steamroll over minorities to make certain that justice is trampled under the jack-booted feet of the oppressors. This nation has been harbouring a nascent pack of fascists for decades, and now they are emboldened and coming out of the woodwork. This is the final nail in the coffin of sanity and justice. Pack up your revolutionary rhetoric and hit the road, and let me get the hell out of your life once and for all. I don't know why I came here to just watch you fail again."

Jesus placed his left hand on Aaron's right shoulder, and smiled with glee. "Aaron, you are here, because you always fight injustice. So stop being a jerk and get with the programme. You are going nowhere, because you always stand against the tyranny of greed."

"You know if I actually believed you are who you say you are, I would demand a seat at your right side in that kingdom in the sky that is supposed to have streets paved with gold."

WHEN JESUS CAME TO THE BLACK HILLS
TO DO THE GHOST DANCE
WITH THE SPIRIT OF SITTING BULL

As they entered the park, the crowd had now swelled to at least 200 or 300 eager people, and Jesus offered an astute observation. "Aaron, you act really tough, but you and I know you have softness in your heart for the downtrodden in a world that is run by and for the privileged. There is no heaven, and we both know it. Heaven is right here, if only people would realize it, and share what they have with one another. All a man needs is provided, but a few think they should have it all. I am about to show the people who have been on their knees for too long that it is time to take back what was stolen, and it was not just land. It was a way of life that was hijacked by the greedy, and even their own leaders, whom they elect to serve them, but serve themselves and bow before the white man while stealing from their own people. Greed is an infectious disease, and I am about to cure it."

Aaron shook his head as pickups, cars and vans began pulling up to the park. Mary and the 12 men who had gone to the ghost dance pulled up and came running toward Jesus. Mary, almost pleading, said, "They have alerted the tribal police, and the FBI, and they are going to arrest you. We need to get you out of here."

"The son of man does not run from the law-enforcement devils of mayhem that represent the establishment."

WHEN JESUS CAME TO THE BLACK HILLS
TO DO THE GHOST DANCE
WITH THE SPIRIT OF SITTING BULL

Aaron, shaking his head said to Mary, "You are wasting your time."

Jesus climbed on top of a picnic table, as maybe 2000 people now gathered in the park. He began to speak. "Brethren of hope, listen to what I say, and prepare to die for the sake of your ancestors, two of whom you saw do the ghost dance with me last night. I tell you that I am not here to bring peace and harmony, but to bring you the sword of righteousness with which you can slay your enemies." He pointed to the east as he continued. "In Washington, D.C. your oppressors turn a blind eye to your plight. Be leery of promises, because promises lie in the dust of your sacred Black Hills, trampled by the evil of greed."

Jesus looked skyward, as if asking some heavenly messenger to send him words. "I come to you with no promise of victory, but I promise you the glorious sanctity of being off your knees, of no longer sitting idly by as the steamroller of lost dreams rolls across your bodies driven by those who see you as sub-human, those who believe in only one God - money. Remember that I once said the worship of money is the root of all evil. I say it again here today, as your very own leaders make their way here as lackeys of those who want to imprison you to their bankrupt greed that is as insidious as the small pox that white men sit loose upon you many years ago. Evil is afoot."

WHEN JESUS CAME TO THE BLACK HILLS
TO DO THE GHOST DANCE
WITH THE SPIRIT OF SITTING BULL

As the tribal police walked into the park, a loud chorus of boos resounded all about. While they approached the picnic table where Jesus was standing, he put forth his two hands in front of his chest.

The six men halted instantly as Jesus said, "You work for those who control your world, those who defile the land of your ancestors. Those you serve are the people who poison the air you breath, contaminate the water you drink and own the food you have to buy for survival. You are the goons for the cretins that crush hope. You are all expected to sanctify greed while the elite steal your savings and use your tax dollars to bail out corporations. You are brainwashed by those who capture the news media and make it servants to the elite who revel in their decadence. They blatantly steal your elections by shoving two parties down your throats that are identical in their devotion to the privileged class. You have helped the power brokers steal this sacred land. You are supporting people who have extinguished the flame of hope."

The tribal police were about to move toward Jesus and pull him down, when they were suddenly surrounded by a band of people with determined looks upon faces that had for too long suffered at the hands of authorities who served their exploiters. Their countenance stayed the six, and they slowly turned and left the park to cheers.

WHEN JESUS CAME TO THE BLACK HILLS
TO DO THE GHOST DANCE
WITH THE SPIRIT OF SITTING BULL

The cheering became almost deafening, as two officers turned and walked back into the crow, standing stoically waiting for Jesus' next oration.

"I am not here to give you respite from sorrow, fear or even physical bondage. I am here to tell you that if you follow me, chances are you will encounter even more sorrow, fear and maybe be incarcerated or even killed. However, none of those things will prevent you from experiencing the exhilaration of freedom from your slavery that has made you victims of injustice for hundreds of years. You may be bloodied in battle, you may be killed in battle, but you will lie on a field of honour here in the sacred Black Hills and know that you did not yield to the evil of those who worship the devil of greed. Go to your homes and get your weapons that the idiots in the NRA believe are your God-given right. Well, we will see what they think of gun control when those guns are in the hands of indignant Native Americans hell-bent on reclaiming their dignity. Moreover, if they send in the military, we will render a defeat on their army that will make Custer's last stand at Little Big Horn seem like child's play. Oh my brethren, I say to you I am the son-of-man, and I come not with words of peace, but with a swift sword that will deliver anarchy."

A mighty roar went up among the throng, and even the tribal police now mingling with the crowd also enthusiastically cheered. Meanwhile, Aaron looked up at Jesus and shook his head. Jesus looked down at him with a smile as he waved his hands asking for quiet. "I say to all of you that we will render an blow to let those in power know we will not accept anything short of total victory. Your days of accepting a piece of paper from a government that has no honour will no longer suffice. We are about to rain down anarchy on those who dare defile the Black Hills. We shall, in the end; all do the ghost dance on the White House lawn if they dare not bend to our will. I can promise you not total victory, but I promise you that when you look at yourself in the mirror, you will not hide your face in shame."

Jesus whispered something to Peter, who left with six of his compatriots. He then continued, as he pointed to Aaron. "My friend, Aaron Adams, is going to help all of us achieve our ends. Be not weary my friends, because I am the light that has come into your darkness, and I will shine a beacon that will either lead you out of the blackness or lead to a last stand against the evil that has plagued you for too long now. The President is an idiot. Most smart people know that – even him, as he is just a frightened little boy in an old man's body who is playing a game of *I am President*. You all saw what happened the last time the rich scion of privilege played that game. George W. Bush nearly destroyed America, and the buffoon in office now is actually far worse. He proves every day that he is nothing but a childish man in search of validation. Well, I am a man in a man's body, and I am not playing. I am anarchy personified."

He paced about for a bit, appearing to be in deep reflective thought as the crowd waited patiently for his next words. "Don't think that this is going to be easy. The President and his government lackeys made up of oil barons, lobbyists for giant corporations and Wall Street tycoons who want to destroy any semblance of compassion are coming after what little you have in a nation with a government that wants all of you to be slaves to the bottom line. Destroying you has been their aim ever since they sit foot on this continent. You are a threat to their greed, because you do not believe man can own shelter, food or land. You see those things as human rights, things that should be shared, not hoarded. These evil representatives of the rich see the land as something they can abuse and poison in their quest for profits. They do not revere it."

He pointed down at an old man standing in the front row. "Waiting to die just got easier with the government this nation currently has. The clock has been running down for a long time. Now, the greedy elite who have been handed the keys to the lock box that kept social programmes safe are coming after your social security. Your Medicare will be robbed, so the rich can get another tax cut. The middle class is through, and they are, in a large part, the very ones who voted for their own deaths by touching the screen for the ones who want to destroy them. Nothing is more pitiful than a man too ignorant to see he is pulling the lever for his own enslavement. Then again, why not? What choices are offered by the two parties that both answer to their corporate masters? The working person loses no matter who is President. Maybe this is just their way of committing suicide."

Aaron sighed, because he knew Jesus was really getting wound up now. He so loved the power of his own words. Jesus continued. "These misguided people are aching. Their backs ache, their heads ache, their hearts ache, their whole lives ache. It is hard for them to get up in the morning and walk the streets hoping for some compassion, but they will not find it in this nation. They are propagandized into believing it is the poor on welfare who are robbing them, when the real robbers are the bankers, the insurance companies, the Wall Street barons of greed and the politicians."

A bright light seemed to form a halo behind him as he continued. "The 99% have to go on, not to live but to die in the throes of misery dispensed by the cruellest economic system ever devised. Each step taken is another step closer to that big black pit the rich, the powerful and the privileged have reserved for the masses. They will push the middle class and poor into that pit while they laugh all the way to the bank. Nothing has changed in thousands of years. This is the modern feudal system where the Lords of the Manor rule with impunity. Corporations are now the kings and queens, the dukes and duchesses who rain down indignity after indignity upon the middle class and poor whom they bind in perpetuity to their evil empires of greed. You, my noble ones, are the last vestige of hope to bring this reign of economic terrorism to a halt."

Jesus slowly and methodically wiped his brow, as his fiery rhetoric was making him work up a tremendous sweat. "You can all join the others who steadfastly refuse to stand against this evil, and just give them the go ahead to push you into that pit of hopelessness, or you can join me, get up off your knees and stop begging for scraps from the table of plenty set for the wealthy and privileged."

He took a deep breath and continued. "I can never promise you victory as the foe has the politicians, the police and the military bound in service to their cause of enslavement. I can assure many of you that the cost of your allegiance to me will be death, but if you let this abomination continue – you are already dead."

CHAPTER 4
JUSTICE IN A NATION THAT HAS NONE

*Then all the Natives cried with one accord,
"Anarchy art King, and God and Lord;
Anarchy, to thee we humbly bow,
Be thy name made holy now!"*

*And Anarchy, in the form of a very pious man,
Was boldly waving his hand over the land.
It was as if all Natives were getting an education
To not meekly bow before the American nation.*

*For Anarchy knew the fake palaces
Of those titans of industry living fallacies;
His the true sceptre, crown, and globe,
He wore not gold, but just a ragged robe.*

J. Wayne Frye 89

WHEN JESUS CAME TO THE BLACK HILLS
TO DO THE GHOST DANCE
WITH THE SPIRIT OF SITTING BULL

So Jesus sent the Natives before,
Telling them it was time to soar.
And he proceeded with determined intent
To allow the Natives their anger to vent.

Jesus was now pacing about as if in a furious rage. He saw the crowd beginning to seethe with fury for all the indignities promulgated by the white man year after year after year. Aaron Adams stood in awe at his mesmerizing power of rhetoric. Aaron was a firm nonbeliever, but he did believe there was something special about the man whom he befriended all those years ago.

One woman stood defiantly, shouting she was tired of being a doormat for the white man. Alas, Jesus said, "The white man's heart is flayed, but you my love should no longer despair. Today there is hope alive in the air. Father time is weak and grey with waiting for that better day. He is tired of seeing how arrogantly America stands with bloodied hands."

Aaron could see that Jesus was about to render the coup de grâce of rhetorical mastery, because his eyes were beaming now as he said, "The rich lie in their palaces of pleasure and the corporations glimmer in the towers of thievery. These entities control your world. They poison the air you breathe so they can reap gross profits. They contaminate the water you drink with their wastes, and provide you with clean water only if you pay for their plastic bottles of thirst quenchers that trickle in more obscene profits to those who sit back and laugh at how stupid you are, how you bow and scrape for a crumb they might toss you from their tables of plenty. They are so mercenary that they even patent and copyright the food you eat, so that your nourishment is another avenue for their profits. They have made you slaves and you don't even realize it. They use their media empires to spread a steady stream of propaganda telling you how wonderful America is and how lucky you are. They have stolen your elections by making sure a person of integrity is never a candidate, always offering you a choice between the lesser of two evils. These are the people who have stolen your lives, and all you do is shrug your shoulders and accept your fate. You sit idly by as they destroy your unions, steal your retirement, ship your sons and daughters off to fight their wars for them, so they can grab more resources while they steal your tax dollars to bail out unending greed. They have stolen your freedom and you don't even realize it. They have bloodied you and destroyed your will to fight. I tell you that I am Jesus come with a mighty sword of retribution. I am no longer the Prince of Peace. I am the Son of Anarchy, and if you get up off your knees and follow me, we will start a revolution that will shake the foundations of the culture of greed and pound it into a pile of rubble."

WHEN JESUS CAME TO THE BLACK HILLS
TO DO THE GHOST DANCE
WITH THE SPIRIT OF SITTING BULL

Aaron knew that the future held great civil discord, because this was a man who relished confrontation. He simply had no fear whatsoever of authority, and though Aaron did not believe in Jesus or anything else from what he called a book of fairy tales, he did believe that Jesus was a man of stellar character who stood by the working men and women who had been destroyed by an oligarchy of the rich and corporations that enslaved them.

Jesus was pacing once again and the crowd waited with anticipatory relish, for they seemed to hang on every word. This was what Jesus did best, stirring people with his words.

Jesus took a deep breath and said, "This morally bankrupt nation has killed Native American hopes and dreams. It has devastated a way of life that stood against their culture of greed. The whites look upon you as heathens, but the real heathens are those who think everything is for sale, that everything has a price tag, that resources are infinite and that the God they worship is superior to all other Gods. These people have killed your grandparents, your parents and now are killing your children. The dust of death is piled high upon your sovereign nation, and they will not be satisfied until they destroy every one of you. However, if you get off your knees they are the ones who will experience the dark side of misery.

Are you ready to join me on the march to your salvation?"

A mighty roar went up from the crowd. Shouting, jumping and dancing, they all were ready to follow this man into hell if he led them there. He had bound them to his cause now with rhetorical mastery. He waved his right hand high and a hush fell over the crowd as he said, "Go to your homes, get any weapons you can find, even if it is only a kitchen knife. We await a grand reckoning and you are all warriors, so put on your war paint as your ancestors did and prepare to die for the sake of righteousness. I shall be here tomorrow morning and we shall, with a force of the mighty defenders, walk into the valley of death, but we will fear no evil for our mighty shields of honour and virtue will protect us."

Jesus noticed a group of white men standing at the back of the park, maybe 100 metres away. They looked suspect. He pointed at them and said, "Those are the same people who 150 years ago served the vile Native American haters who sat out to destroy your ancestors. These are the descendants of George Armstrong Custer. They are the government lackeys who serve a foreign power in the White House. Ah, but they are about to meet the same fate as Custer who tasted the wrath of an aroused Indian Nation." He then looked at those six men and pointing his finger directly at them, continued, "You spawn of arrogance and hatred are welcome to join us. You are welcome to throw aside your devotion to the evil of those who sit in judgment and arrogance as they pursue more land and more resources to satisfy their greed. I know you will not do so, because you are like so many who serve the privileged of this nation. Your first duty is to maintain your own seat at the table of power, in the belief that you are part of the privileged class. You are not. You are just lackeys used by the powerful to exert their control. You are devouring your own flesh in service to those who hand you a morsel from their table of plenty and enslave you. You are more disgusting than the powerful and wealthy you serve, because you have no self-respect, you have no depth of character and you are lost souls in the desert of manipulation and control that has imprisoned you."

One of the men, tall, maybe 6:4, started to reach inside his coat, but Jesus pointed his finger at him and smiling said, "Do not be foolish. Your gun cannot kill but a few of us, and it can never kill the idea of justice for all in a nation that wallows in oppression. Go back to your Washington bosses and tell them you witnessed an uprising of conscience among a people who have been oppressed too long. Tell them that the Prince of Anarchy is among the natives, and he is stirring up a rebellion that will light a fire which will consume these sanctified Black Hills unless these noble people are afforded the dignity they have been denied for so long."

The crowd began to move toward the six men, but Jesus, raising his right hand again, signifying a stopping motion, said, "Do not harm these men now. The time for war is not here yet. We shall offer an olive branch, but if it is rejected, we will grab a mighty oak branch and use it to bludgeon your oppressors."

The men retreated slowly and Aaron, looking at Jesus, knew he was in the middle of a fire storm, and that with Jesus, the end would probably not be pleasant, because he had seen what happened the previous times when he stood with this exceptional man against the forces of evil. Still, he was strangely drawn to him, because Aaron had always been a champion of the oppressed, a believer in the dignity of the poor, the downtrodden and the forgotten.

Jesus was not through with his oratory. He looked out into the huge throng of people as the crowd had grown to well over 3000 now. "For too long, you have all bowed to the oppressor. Those who control the government in this land have no idea how empty their own souls are. The Statue of Liberty that stands boldly in New York Harbour is barren. She gasps for air fouled by the pollution of greed. Under the skin no longer beats a heart, because the arteries of democracy that used to flow through her veins have been severed to serve the interests of the privileged. She is hung up bloodily, eyes bulging, like some gutted cow at the slaughter pen. Only the hook is invisible. A dark shadow is cast over the land blotting out the sunshine of justice. The masses have been inside lady liberty and horror of horrors – they now know she is empty."

The crowd was enthralled, absorbing every single word. "I tell each and every one of you that you are the last hope for justice in a nation that long ago lost its way. All of you who are tired of being a doormat for the wealthy barons of greed must arise from your supplication. You must stop being the pawns of the privileged class that think they are special by virtue of birth. You must never again bow in supplication before the arrogant government bureaucrats who serve the interests of corporations. I am a raving revolutionary, and you all must become revolutionaries or continue to be irrevocably bound by the chains of misery that imprison you."

The word revolutionary was particularly stirring to the crowd. There was something magical about it, something that titillated the soul of the oppressed. It was the gold that sparkled in the dark chambers of lost hope.

WHEN JESUS CAME TO THE BLACK HILLS
TO DO THE GHOST DANCE
WITH THE SPIRIT OF SITTING BULL

Jesus had the immense crowd in the palm of his hand with his spellbinding oratory. They were aroused with indignation, as he sowed the seeds of revolution against evil.

Wilfully, he said, "The revolutionary must fight against the winds of tyranny. The revolutionary is the last barrier that keeps the capitalists at bay. The revolutionary is the last hope for society to emerge from the dungeon of darkness and despair into the bright sunshine of justice and equality. The voices of the forgotten and disenfranchised crying out for justice must be heeded. The evil of greed must be exposed, so it can no longer hide in the squalor and filth of darkness, turning its back on the plight of the masses who must beg for scraps from the tables of plenty. It is the duty of the revolutionary to summon a wind so powerful and strong that it will blow across the land like a vindictive cyclone to demolish the corrupt houses of the capitalists into a pile of rubble. The evil wall of discontent these greedy ghouls have constructed shall not deter the righteous revolutionaries who will make justice and freedom reign across the barren land of broken promises. The first step begins tonight at the council meeting where we will demand they stand up to their white masters in Washington and finally earn the salaries and benefits they have voted themselves. Be there ready to demand they represent you, rather than themselves."

WHEN JESUS CAME TO THE BLACK HILLS
TO DO THE GHOST DANCE
WITH THE SPIRIT OF SITTING BULL

The council meeting was in a small hall that seated no more than 100 people, but the council got wind of what had occurred at Bear Butte and Two Moccasins Park. Worried about what would ensue in an open meeting, they put up a sign on the door that read *Closed Session*. The sign was ripped down, and two burly men busted open the locked door as hundreds piled in while a couple of thousand stood outside. The tribal police, who had been called out to guard the council, tried to stop the onslaught of people to no avail, finally giving up after Jesus stared them down as they started to draw their weapons. "Draw those at your own peril. These people are not in the mood to acquiesce to any threats from the representatives of the establishment. Stop doing the white man's bidding and start serving the people you have sworn to protect."

The chief started banging his gavel and Jesus moved to the banister that was a barrier used to cordon off the people from their representatives. Like the white man's government that always erected a barrier between the people and its representatives, the Native Americans had utilized the same techniques to keep the people separated from their government. Jesus stood there defiant and proud as he addressed the chief and council. "You can bang that gavel all you want, but it will not quiet the anger that has built within the hearts and minds of the Lakota people. You can lead them into a brighter day or they will replace you with those who are warriors of indignation ready to demand justice from the U.S. government. The choice is yours. The son of man wants no position, wants no aggrandizement and wants nothing from you but the fulfillment of your duties to the people of this great native nation. I am but a catalyst that has aroused the people to take a stand against the injustices of hundreds of years. This is the dawn of a new day. You can embrace the sunshine of hope with us, or you can remain in the darkness and cower in fear before the behemoth of evil that is the United States government."

The chief and council looked quizzically at one another, and the many years of self-serving fear seemed to flow into a raging torrent of indignant, rousing, redemptive wrath. They stood up, raised their fists and shouted in unison, "We are with the people."

Aaron, standing to the far left of Jesus, could not believe how this charismatic man could so thoroughly arouse people with his fiery rhetoric. In a couple of days, he had quelled years of apathy and lit a spark that was becoming a raging inferno. Jesus winked at him and whispered, "Damn, I'm good!"

Mary, now a nearly constant companion of Aaron, smiled at him and said, "Have you ever seen anyone like him? I am a non-believer, but there is something mystical about this man."

"I have been here before Mary. You are right, but no matter how much you believe in him you also have to believe in the power of all the forces arrayed against him. The rich and powerful are too entrenched to be dislodged. They have captured this country and will never yield power peacefully. He stands no chance against the vast resources and power of the American military and police that serve the interests of the wealthy. I have seen him defeated twice and the end will not be pleasant."

She reached down and took Aaron's hand, squeezed it gently and said, "Well, regardless of how it turns out, at least I met you."

Aaron sighed and replied, "Mary, I am a washed-up old man. You can do better."

"Aaron, I see how Jesus adores you, and if he sees the good in you, believe me, it is an acclamation of your worth as a human being. He saw the good in me, despite my alcoholism and my past as a prostitute. I have no belief in God, but that man's kindness and faith in me has made me be reborn. I am ready to move forward and make my life meaningful. I will follow him into the fires of hell, and despite your scepticism, I know you will too."

WHEN JESUS CAME TO THE BLACK HILLS
TO DO THE GHOST DANCE
WITH THE SPIRIT OF SITTING BULL

Aaron felt a surge of hormones as he looked down at a woman who showed more than her 34 years, but harboured a quiet sensuality that was arousing passions in Aaron that he thought had died long ago. He felt a rise between his legs.

Mary, looking down at what was happening, said, "Old maybe, but definitely not dead."

As the crowd dispersed, Jesus sat in conference with the council, instructing them on what his plans were. Peter came into the chambers with a group of burly looking white and black men with determined looks upon their faces, maybe twenty in number, ranging in age from the twenties to mid-fifties. Jesus motioned for Aaron and Mary to take a seat with him and the council as he said, "Come my friends, there are plans to be made." The men who came in with Peter moved to the council table and took a seat on the floor.

Aaron and Mary sat on the floor with the men who seemed to possess military precision in their movements. Jesus took a deep breathe and said, as he pointed to Aaron. "This is my right arm of justice, Aaron Adams, and I tell you all that he will never fail the cause of righteousness, for he may be a non-believer in my divinity, and in God, himself, but he is a believer in the sanctity of man and his compassion for the downtrodden is renowned and he never trembles before authority.

The day may come when once again I am killed as I have been many times in many places, but always remember that you can kill a man, but you cannot kill an idea."

He pointed at a determined-looking grey haired man sitting on the floor, muscular with broad shoulders and a stern bearing. "This is Colonel Barton, retired U.S. Army Green Beret, and the men with him are his loyal comrades in arms. They are all tired of doing the dirty work of making nations bow before the corporate war machine. They are going to teach our warriors the art of guerrilla warfare, because although we do not want it, if push comes to shove, we will no longer be pushed."

Aaron was worried now. Encouraging this type of action meant Jesus was about to kick a hornets' nest filled with stinging anti-bodies in Washington, D.C., and just how was Jesus going to stand against the mightiest army the world had ever known. The President had no heart, no soul and no patience for anything that stood in the way of the oligarchy that had seized the USA, making it a bastion of intolerance for anything but white men making their last stand against the people of colour whom the President saw as usurpers of the natural order of things. Death and destruction lay ahead if Jesus initiated an anarchical war against the establishment.

WHEN JESUS CAME TO THE BLACK HILLS
TO DO THE GHOST DANCE
WITH THE SPIRIT OF SITTING BULL

Jesus could see the worry on Aaron's face, and said, "There was a time in this nation when there was a prescription for the poor, when the government could write a prescription for a poor man that simply said we will help you get a job, save money, pull yourself up from despair, but that dream died with Ronald Reagan's culture of greed. Too many Americans are ignorant to the experiences of the truly poor. These are the people who sell tools at Sears, and fix roofs, and take care of the elderly, mow lawns and serve meals. They're not getting a living wage. There's no money left at the end of the week for them to save. There's nothing left if they get sick. Nothing left if their car breaks down. And if they make a mistake, there's nothing left to pay fines or fees. The system kicks dirt in the faces of the poor. You can't pull yourself up when there's nothing to grab onto. The American dream has become an American nightmare, and I am going to foment anarchy to bring these arrogant oligarchs to their knees if they do not bow before the real Americans who want to be able to live in peace, free of the culture of greed."

Aaron sighed. "As always, your ambitions are noble my friend, but the truth is the battle for economic fairness has been lost. The rich won. I mean look at who is running the country now. Far too many of the poor sit at home and don't vote, and why should they? The state governments erect barriers to voting, and even if the poor did vote, look at the choices they are offered. There is not a dimes worth of difference between the two parties, and third parties have no chance, because they have no money and no avenues to get out their message."

Smiling, Jesus stood and looking at Colonel Barton, said, "How long can a guerrilla army survive in this nation?"

"This nation is vast and a guerrilla army cannot defeat the American army militarily, but it can harass, attack with small mobile forces against a large, unwieldy military machine that relies on weapons of mass destruction. The USA has not won a war since World War II, because it has two things working against it – reliance on superior technology rather than well-trained cadres of devoted fighters, and it has, in almost every case, been fighting for riches and devotion to capitalism rather than commitment to the people. Thus, guerrilla forces with far less firepower, but much more devotion to a cause have defeated them. The guerrilla force is largely or entirely organized in small units that are dependent on the support of the local population. Tactically, the guerrilla army makes repetitive attacks far from the opponent's center of gravity with a view to keeping its own casualties to a minimum and imposing a constant debilitating strain on the enemy. This may provoke the enemy into a brutal, excessively destructive response, which will both anger their own supporters and increase support for the guerrillas, ultimately compelling the enemy to withdraw or settle with the opposing force. The American defeat in Vietnam proved the validity of guerrilla warfare. Ho Chi Minh defeated the mightiest army ever assembled simply because that army was not only fighting for an unjust cause, but because that army was too large and unwieldy to engage the enemy with precision. Superior manpower and firepower does not assure victory. The idiot sitting in the Oval Office now will throw everything he has at any insurgency, but in the end that strategy will lead to chaos."

Aaron, who had fought valiantly in the lost cause of Vietnam, knew the Colonel was right, but he feared for all the innocents who would suffer, because the man in the White House had no compassion, no heart, no soul. All he worshipped was his own image, and he relished being a grand leader in making America great, when, in fact, America had been in steady decline and was poised for an even more precipitous drop with the take over of government by the oligarchy which was determined to destroy the last vestige of fairness in a system that aggrandized greed. In deep thought about this, Aaron realized that maybe the Colonel was on to something. "You are right. You cannot win militarily, but you can create such havoc that the people, the majority of whom voted against this buffoon, will begin to rally to the cause, and in the end, the mighty may realize there is no way out but to settle. However, what frightens me most is the idiot who is now in charge would have no qualms about nuking the entire Black Hills. He is a lunatic, a man with no heart, no soul and no conscience."

Jesus, realizing that Aaron was now beginning to embrace the cause, said, "Yes, and it is a gamble we must take, because these noble people are better off dead than bowing to the greed that permeates the very heart of America. When the last tree is cut, when the last river is poisoned, when the sacred Black Hills fall before the bulldozer, life ceases to have meaning for these people, anyway."

Aaron now knew what his job was, as he addressed Jesus. "You want me to stall while you prepare for anarchy. You want me to be your shill, try to prolong the ultimate conflict which will occur, you hope, only when you are ready to confront the government with anarchy so complete and total in scope that they will bend before committing troops to quill the rebellion of the Lakota people."

"You speak well my friend, but it has been a long day, let us all seek repose so that we may awaken refreshed and ready for the coming battle. Tomorrow begins the preparations for a war that will decide the fate of the Lakota people."

All filed out and started for cars and trucks, but Jesus paused, winked at Aaron and Mary, as he said, "I shall sleep with my brethren. I think you two need to get to know one another better."

Mary bowed her head, but Jesus reached down and lifted her chin. "You have found a good man. Just remember I need him, so make sure he doesn't have a heart attack. He is old, and I think I may have forgotten how to raise the dead."

Laughing, they parted company. Aaron and Mary strolled down the street toward Aaron's hotel. Despite the fact that liaisons with men were commonplace for Mary, she felt timid.

Aaron could sense Mary's trepidation about what was seemingly on the horizon between them. "Mary, I do not care about what you have done before. People do what they must to survive. The world is a cruel place run by cruel people who spend far too much time judging others rather than looking in the mirror. I can see the goodness in you and the compassion that you have."

She smiled, took his hand and they strolled to the hotel, where Aaron became the one experiencing trepidation. At one time, he was the stud of Manhattan, but those days were long behind him now. The tingle he used to get between his legs in the presence of a beautiful woman – hey, almost any woman – was now reduced to nothing more than a twitch that quickly dissipated into the deep recesses of old age. Still, he was feeling something with Mary that he had not felt in a long time.

Mary's life had been on a steady downhill descent for as long as she could remember. The drugs, the booze, the men, the lost jobs, lost family and lost hope had taken a toll. However, she was like a rose that had wilted, then as the morning dew gently caressed the petals and the sunlight bathed it in warmth, there was a reawakening, a shine that glistened in the brightness of a new day. Was Aaron her new day?

Aaron had always been smooth with women, and despite his diminishing virility, that had not faded. Women were still mesmerized by his calm, cool, assured manner. He pointed toward the shower and said, "You can go first."

Mary got up, meandered very nonchalantly over to Aaron, smiled coyly, took Aaron by the hand and gently tugged him along with her to the bathroom. Aaron's breathing quickened as a surge of reminiscing about past sexual liaisons were flashing like a kaleidoscope through his mind? Was he up for the occasion? As he felt the bulge grow in his pants, to his surprise, the answer was yes.

Mary and Aaron lovingly fondled one another in the shower and lingered for what seemed an hour kissing, touching and groping the places that sent shivers though their bodies. They moved to the bed, and Aaron felt a surge of pride as he had a solid, rock hard erection, which made her grin as she crawled between his legs. She blew gently on his member and then licked it from scrotum to tip. Aaron moaned as he felt her warm wet mouth engulf his rock hard passion pole all the way down to his huge balls.

Mary moaned loudly around his massive erection, sending multiple vibrations all through Aaron's body, and into his pulsating member. She whispered, "I love its taste. I love its length. I love its girth, and I am going to love swallowing your joy juice."

Then she furiously dove back down, taking him all the way down her throat and held him there as she sucked like a vacuum cleaner with her lips and jaws. She started swallowing, making her mouth pump the head while squeezing his pulsating balls as if she was trying to prime a pump for a huge explosion of liquid.

WHEN JESUS CAME TO THE BLACK HILLS
TO DO THE GHOST DANCE
WITH THE SPIRIT OF SITTING BULL

Aaron let out a slow, methodical moan as he squirted his essence down her throat. She guzzled it down like a champion. She continued sucking to get every drop she could. When there simply was nothing left to squirt, she blew on it with her hot breath and licked the head with her tongue

She smiled and crawled up into his arms, nestling there beside him. Unbelievably, the 65 year old Aaron, as she reached down to fondle his member, rose to the occasion again. Mary stared down at it and said, "My, oh my, aren't we the stud tonight?" She crawled in top of him and rubbed her hairy crotch across his chest as she worked her way to his face where she buried him in the sweet nectar of her womanhood. Aaron's tongue darted upward and she began to moan while writhing rhythmically back and forth on his soft, darting tongue.

He started licking up and down from the top to the bottom. He plunged in deeper and deeper, burying his face in her essence. He sucked her swollen clit into his mouth and lightly nibbled on it. She was bucking her hips up at the same time as he was frantically licking while grabbing and squeezing her shapely, soft ass cheeks.

When she had finished her gigantic orgasm, Aaron flipped her over onto her belly. He saw her little brown hole and gently pushed his huge member against it. She shouted, "Ram it Aaron, ram it hard, baby."

He kept slamming harder and faster into her tightness as she reached under her elevated hips and massaged his balls, as if she wanted to squeeze his joy juice out of it. Suddenly he exploded, spraying the nectar of the gods deep inside her, as she had another orgasm.

They lay there for a while with his member still inside her, pulsating. He backed out of her and they rolled into each other's arms, falling to sleep in blissfulness.

Real sex is like a wind that howls and roars, sets you ablaze, makes you burn through the skies and ignite the night like a bright star. Real sex born from affection cuts you loose with the will to do what it takes to solidify the relationship, no matter what it costs you. Real affection scorches you like a wildfire and you can't stop running simply because you keep on burning everything that you touch due to the intensity of your passion. If you don't feel that, if you can't embrace the will to light a candle that burns at both ends and meets in the middle to spark a blaze that devours the two of you in a roaring inferno, then you have experienced transitory lust only, not the abiding, deep-rooted affection that says, "I want to spend eternity in your arms, feeling your warmth that embraces me in the glory of a world that is aglow with the light of hope."

These two, in the most unlikely of places had climbed the mountain to Nirvana, and they awoke the next morning to another fervent round of passion. As they lay naked on the bed, there was a knock at the door, and a soft voice said, "If you two can dampen your passionate ardour for awhile, I would like to talk."

Aaron put a towel around himself and went to the door as Mary pulled the covers over her body. Jesus, walking in smiling, said, "Looks like the two of you were on the war path of love last night. Unfortunately, you will have to curb your passion, as I need the two of you to go to the Bureau of Indian Affairs in Aberdeen and tell them the Black Hills were ceded to these people in perpetuity – only don't use that word, as I doubt the idiots understand it. Make it clear that we have one set of demands and if not met, there will be no peace and the USA will have a war on its hands like no other this nation has ever undertaken, and Mr. Fire and Fury, as the President likes to call himself, had better prepare for a bit of fire and fury to be used against this nation."

Jesus reached very determinedly into his back pocket and brought out a folded sheet of bond paper. He handed it to Aaron, who read it aloud:

WHEN JESUS CAME TO THE BLACK HILLS
TO DO THE GHOST DANCE
WITH THE SPIRIT OF SITTING BULL

To: Leland Abercrombie, Dakota Director of BIA
From: The Lakota People
Subject: Our Sacred Black Hills and an Ultimatum to Cease and Desist in the Continued Abrogation of Treaties Signed by the U.S.A.

My dear Mr. Abercrombie, Director of the B.I.A. in Aberdeen, South Dakota, please be cognizant of the fact that if the below demands are not met by Friday May 1st, a state of war shall exist between the Lakota Nation and the United States of America. We are prepared for a war of attrition, which you cannot win, so heed the demands or face the consequences.

1. We hereby claim all rights afforded the Lakota people under the Fort Laramie Treaties of 1851 and 1868 and firmly reject the Sioux Appropriation Bill of 1876, which was passed by Congress but never agreed to by the Lakota Nation.

2. We firmly reject the Congressional Act of 1877, which illegally appropriated additional lands without approval of the Lakota Nation. The same applies to the 1899 Congressional Dawes Act which opened 9 million acres of confiscated land to white settlers.

3. We reject the 1910 Sioux Reservation Act, again passed without Lakota signatories. We demand the return of all property confiscated under that act.

4. The one billion dollars we were awarded by the Supreme Court in the USA vs. the Sioux Nation Case remains unclaimed, because our land was not and never will be for sale. That is the white man's way. It is not the Lakota way to own the Mother Earth. The one billion dollars has been unclaimed for nearly 40 years and will remain so.

The USA has consistently refused to negotiate in good faith with the Lakota people. Today, that must end. Our demands are not negotiable. We have waited too long to be treated fairly, and will no longer tolerate a foreign presence on our lands without permission from the rightful owners, the Lakota people. We hereby demand complete and total adherence to the Ft. Laramie Treaty of 1868. You have until the aforementioned May 1 to agree, or the result will be a declaration of war by the Lakota Nation against the U.S. government.
Sincerely,
Jesus – Representative of the Lakota People

Aaron looked down at Mary, back at Jesus, took a deep breath and said, "Damn, if I had any sense I'd walk away and never look back."

Jesus smiled and replied, "You can't do that Aaron, because you believe in justice, real justice in a nation that has none."

CHAPTER 5
THEN YOU BETTER
COME WELL-ARMED

*Anarchy bade they all lay down in the street,
Right before American soldiers trampling feet,
Expecting with an assured and determined eye
Fraud, genocide and indifference to now defy.*

*Alas between Anarchy and his foes
A mist, a light, an image rose,
Small at first, and weak and frail.
Like the vapour of the vale.*

*Till, as clouds grew on the blast,
Injuns shouted "the foe is striding fast,"
And lightning bolts were let fly,*

WHEN JESUS CAME TO THE BLACK HILLS
TO DO THE GHOST DANCE
WITH THE SPIRIT OF SITTING BULL

As natives spoke in thunder from the sky.

The snake is a loathsome creature, but it is representative of the evil that slithers about in the hearts and minds of those who sit on thrones of gold embossed with the blood of a noble race. The snake symbolizes disease, weakness and malice, which is the chronic malady of the majority of Americans. Of course, everybody knows the symbol of success in American is the huge bull that is emblematic of a robust stock market, which is what really matters to the wealthy class. Today, the only real nourishment that is offered by the wealthy to the masses is already half digested by the cretins who hunger for more and more but can never be satisfied.

In the grand scheme of things, people are nothing in America. They are but resources to grease the machinery of capitalism. Native Americans made a big mistake when they extended the hand of friendship to the arriving pilgrims. That hand was bitten off by a pack of self-righteous hypocrites much like today's Jesus-loving, finger pointing, condemning, arrogant, self-righteous paragons of virtue who would not know compassion if it bit them on the ass. Hypocrisy is a seed that was planted long ago in the USA, and it has sprouted into a huge tree with branches that hide the sunlight of hope from all who live under the propagandized vision of how grand the nation is that has no heart or soul when it comes to the way the least among the masses are treated. There is no hand up extended by the uncaring government that serves the oligarchy or by the Christians that prey rather than pray!

America is not a land of opportunity, but rather a land of opportunists. When a man robs a 7-11 with gun in hand to feed his hungry children, he will get a long stretch in the slammer. When a man behind a bank desk robs a family of their home with the stroke of a pen, he is rewarded with a pat on the back, a promotion and a generous bonus.

This is the way of a nation where people get the best government they can buy, and the U.S. government long ago sold out Native Americans to real estate speculators, railroads, oil companies and mining interests. The business of America is business, and heaven help anyone who stands in the way of a corporation, because the Constitution may say government of the people, by the people and for the people, but the truth is that America is a nation where the purpose of government is to serve the moneyed interests.

Aaron knew the truth about America, and that was why Jesus wanted him by his side. He saw through the hypocrisy of a nation more concerned about someone not standing for the National Anthem than for a child going to bed hungry. This type of uncaring government was actually supported by the very people who were crushed under its jack-booted feet of authoritarianism. Yet, they gobbled up the propaganda and embraced it in the fervent belief that they were living in the greatest nation on earth.

In Aberdeen, as Aaron walked from his rental car with Mary, she reached down and lovingly took his hand, very gently squeezing it in what felt almost like desperation. The warmth of Aaron's hand made her feel safe with him. In a near whisper, with deep trepidation in her voice, she said, "People are going to die aren't they?"

"Yes Mary, justice is not achieved without a high cost, because those who have the reins of power will never give up their privilege without a determined fight. They will sit in their golden towers of affluence and order others to carry out the defence of their privilege, and there are always those willing to defend the privileged class. The very people who are trampled by the privileged far too often vote for their oppressors out of the belief that one party loves Jesus more than the other or will protect their right to walk around carrying AK-47's in Wal-Mart. Never underestimate the stupidity of the American voter."

One of the wealthiest individuals in the state of South Dakota was the arrogant man sitting behind the desk at the Aberdeen, South Dakota Bureau of Indian Affairs Office. Leland Abercrombie had been appointed by the buffoon calling himself the President, because they were both major stockholders in an oil pipeline that was now working its way across the Black Hills and Pine Ridge without any concern for the scared land that it threatened to inundate with the black ooze of greed that was pumped out of the ground to feed the avaricious appetites of the barons who ruled the nation with no reverence for the land they defiled in search of black gold. He had no interest in seeing Aaron, as when told by his secretary a man named Adams had an important message for him, he said, "I have a golf date to make. Have my assistant see him. He can't be that important."

The secretary said, "He may not be important, but he is a man with a history of causing trouble."

The director eased back into his chair and seemed to contemplate as he said, "Aaron Adams you say. That name – that name."

"Yes sir. That name should ring a bell, because of what happened in New Jersey and Canada. He aided some nut-job calling himself Jesus in both places and all hell ensued."

"Oh yeah, I remember now. Maybe it would be wise to see him so we can size up his intentions."

"Excellent idea sir. I'll show him and the lady with him in."

While all this was going on, Jesus was huddling with Colonel Barton and his men, laying the groundwork to let justice roll down like raging waters of righteousness into a whirlpool of mayhem. They both knew that the liar-in-chief who sat in the Oval Office understood that the power of a well-crafted lie was as light as a feather and would go around so swiftly it would take people's breath away. In fact, the new President had refined lying into an art form and a large segment of the population embraced his lies with great fervour. On the other hand, the truth had to hire an express train to pull it out of a station of suspicions planted by those who had mastered the art of patriotic propaganda used to manipulate the ignorant masses into swallowing the lies about living in the greatest nation on earth. People were simply too busy standing with pride to honour a National Anthem that glorifies war and sanctifies slavery to realize they were dupes in a grand scheme by the privileged class to use patriotism to enslave them. The Pledge of Allegiance recited every morning in schools across America is not about honouring the nation as much as it is about using it as a tool to effectively brainwash impressionable young minds into blind patriotism, so that they will one day gladly line-up to be cannon fodder for the military industrial complex that gives the rich a pass on military service while the poor blindly and patriotically wave the flag and proudly march across the world to enslave more and more people to American capitalistic ideology.

Colonel Barton and his loyal men had once been part of that abomination. However, they had returned from wars in foreign lands to see the misery of American capitalism, as it allowed more and more of its citizens to sink into poverty while allowing obscene benefits to accrue to those at the top of the economic ladder. They were repulsed by the only first world nation that did not guarantee healthcare to all, and they were dismayed by the lack of social amenities for people. They could no longer idly stand by as a nation was turned over lock, stock and barrel to be plundered by the privileged class. They had met Jesus in Canada, where plans were laid for them to come to Pine Ridge and assist in what would be a great uprising among the Lakota people, an uprising that would gradually encompass all tribes who for too long had been trampled on by a government that stole their land along with their way of life. This was not just about reclaiming their heritage. This was about retribution for all the wrongs promulgated by a racist nation that saw non-whites and non-Christians as heathens befouling the great march of progress that made the earth a commodity to be exploited.

WHEN JESUS CAME TO THE BLACK HILLS
TO DO THE GHOST DANCE
WITH THE SPIRIT OF SITTING BULL

Colonel Barton and his brave men represented that extremely rare breed of militarily trained individuals who effectively analyzed the real reasons behind so many American wars. It was not to defend freedom, but to defend the right of the capitalistic captains of industry to profit from war. Barton and his men were now aligning themselves with a man whom they saw as the only hope for an America lost in self-aggrandizement and self-glorification that blinded most people to the truth. They saw the Lakota people as a way to rise up against the evil that was slowly strangling a nation to death.

Peter Running Bear and Bartholomew Soaring Eagle showed up at the meeting, which was taking place in the dry ravine near Wounded Knee Creek. With them were hundreds of well-armed young men of the tribe who were ready to train with Colonel Barton and his Green Berets as they readied for a raid on the National Guard Armoury in Rapid City. There, they would commandeer tanks, machine guns, mortars and artillery pieces and transport them to Wounded Knee where they were going to set up a defensive perimeter around the church where the 1973 stand-off had occurred.

Also, with Peter and Bartholomew were a cadre of Lakota trained to fly the General Dynamic F-16 Fighting Falcon aircraft. For a year, they had been training in Iran, preparing for this day. These were the brightest and best of the Lakota nation, and they all knew the day would come when they would be compared to the 9/11 hijackers, but they also knew no real progress was made by dropping to your knees and begging for your rights. All Martin Luther King's marches, all he pleas he made for justice were ignored. It was not he who motivated the power structure's embrace of justice. Rather, it was the Black Panthers and the rioters burning down ghettos, which made the white power structure realize their suburban enclaves of privilege would be next for destruction. Only then, with cities in flames, did they realize that a bone had to be tossed to the people who had tired of injustice and were rising up in unison. That was why long before Jesus arrived at Pine Ridge, he had coordinated plans for this day of retribution and sat things in motion to make it possible to shock the establishment with one swift bold move. Along with the raiders, these pilots were going to commandeer aircraft from the Air Guard base in Sioux Falls.

As these revolutionaries talked, a huge landing field was being prepared near Crestview Butte, where the planes would be housed under camouflage until needed. These bold moves were all unfolding as Aaron walked into Leland Abercrombie's office. He did not say a word. He simply handed Abercrombie the letter written by Jesus.

Abercrombie read it and a scowl slowly grew across his lips. He threw it down on the desk and shouted, "Treasonous!"

Aaron, very calmly replied, as he pointed to a chair where Mary sat down. "Treason? How can you commit treason against a nation that does not live up to its treaties? The Lakota people have been very patient with the USA, but apparently, their patience is at an end. I am nothing but a messenger for a man calling himself Jesus. You have the demands there, and he is giving you, thanks to my urging, more time to think than he originally wanted to give. You have one week."

"One week? You haul your ass back to that hovel where those cretins live in squalor and tell this self-proclaimed messiah that this nation has a real commander and chief now. We'll send in the army and destroy the reservation if necessary. We will not permit anyone to defy the law of the land."

"You have been defying the law of the land for over 100 years. The very treaties signed by the U.S. government are the law of the land. I suggest you tell that buffoon who is playing at being President that he is up against more than a pack of unorganized Native Americans. These people have been aroused by a charismatic figure who has convinced them that he has resurrected the spirits of Sitting Bull and Crazy Horse, and I can tell you from experience that you may well win in the end, but you are going against a man and a people who are going to fight brutality with brutality."

"Fight? These backward packs of drunken, lazy malcontents have no fight left in them. They all have their hands out, expecting the government to support them."

Aaron, getting perturbed now, replied, "Well, I tell you what. Maybe if you took 10% of the hand outs by the government to rich assholes like you and shared it with them, they would have no reason to rebel."

Abercrombie rose from behind his desk and said, "I have worked hard to get where I am."

That was it for Aaron. "Listen you bombastic asshole. I know about the history of you and your family. You started out as a vice-president in daddy's company just like your bothers and sisters. None of you would know what work meant if it came up and bit you on the ass. You all have had things handed to you all your life, but degrade those stuck in poverty as if poverty was a disease. Well, it is a disease, a contagious disease that people like you spread because of your greed. Now, I delivered the letter as instructed. Share it with that other scion of privilege sitting in the

White House. He can communicate with Jesus in his usual way with 140 characters on Twitter if he wants. I doubt if he has the intellectual capacity to understand what is in the letter, but tell him that he is messing with the same man who wrecked havoc in Woodbury, New Jersey and the Broughton Archipelago. This man lost both those battles, but there was mass destruction because of the government and the church not negotiating with him. I am telling you that this will not end pleasantly. Mark my words, this is a battle you may win, but the cost will be astronomical."

"Out, and tell that false messiah that we are coming for him"

Aaron motioned for Mary to get up. He took a deep breath and said, "Then you better come well-armed."

CHAPTER 6
A BIG DOSE OF JUSTICE

*On its helm, seen far away,
A vision, in the mind's eye lay;
And those plumes of light rained through
Like a shower of crimson dew.*

*With step as soft as wind it passed
O'er the heads of American soldiers so fast
That they knew the presence of fear there,
And looked up at the undulating air.*

*As Natives beneath the footstep waken,
As stars from night's loose hair are shaken,
As waves arise when loud winds call,
Fear sprung wherever that step did fall.*

WHEN JESUS CAME TO THE BLACK HILLS
TO DO THE GHOST DANCE
WITH THE SPIRIT OF SITTING BULL

And the soldiers, thousands in multitude
Fell as if lances pierced them deep in blood,
Hope, beside anarchy most serene,
Was now slaying the American fiend.

Ah, with a sword, Anarchy, of ghastly birth,
Lay death after death upon America's earth;
The Horse of Death, tame-less as wind
Pranced and white arrogance could not grin.

Jesus was amazed as into the Pine Ridge Reservation was pouring hundreds of former soldiers in America's army of foreign conquest, and they were there to right the wrongs they had promulgated through participation in unjust wars. They were all well-armed with automatic weapons in a nation that glorified guns, and now the very people who fought for the right of all citizens to walk around packing AK-47 assault rifles were about to see their folly used against them.

Jesus stood among the gathering crowd, reaching out with both hands to greet those who had decided they had simply had enough of hypocrisy and were going to stand with their Native American brothers and sisters against injustice. White, brown and black former soldiers mingled with natives in a swelling manifestation of mutual respect as they prepared to go up against the world's biggest terrorist organization – the U.S. government.

WHEN JESUS CAME TO THE BLACK HILLS
TO DO THE GHOST DANCE
WITH THE SPIRIT OF SITTING BULL

Aaron had just arrived back from Aberdeen with Mary, and as he watched Jesus mount a picnic table to speak to the crowd, he nodded at him, letting him know he had completed his task as assigned. Aaron reached down and took Mary's hand. He whispered to her, "Get ready. He is about to deliver the coup de grâce of rhetorical mastery. I do not believe he is the real Jesus, because I do not believe in any Jesus. However, I do believe there is something special about this man, something that touches the hearts and minds of those who desperately need a saviour, someone who can lead them out of the wilderness of despair almost everyone in this country lives in, because it is run by and for those at the top of the economic ladder. I am here, because he has a power over me I cannot explain, but I know in my heart that this will end badly. I have seen it before. He actually thinks people will be more concerned about justice than about who won the latest *American Idol*, what those media whores the Kardashians are doing, what the scores of the football or basketball games are. He can't understand that people have been brainwashed into accepting their own mediocrity by a world where technology has made them into modern-day slaves. Yet, he has picked the Lakota this time – the poorest of the poor in a nation that allows the most obscene poverty in the world among plenty. Maybe these people are the spark he needs to light a fire that will rage across this nation and consume it in righteousness."

WHEN JESUS CAME TO THE BLACK HILLS
TO DO THE GHOST DANCE
WITH THE SPIRIT OF SITTING BULL

Mary sighed and said, "I believe in him Aaron. I do not believe in the Biblical Jesus either, but for some unknown reason, I do believe in this man."

Jesus raised his right hand with a sweeping motion and all there were instantly quiet as he began to speak. "The idle rich lie in their palaces of excess and the corporation executives prance about in their two-thousand dollar suits in their glimmering towers of opulence while plotting how to steal more and more from gullible consumers who think happiness has a price tag. These are the same people whose ancestors carved up this land upon which we stand and called it real estate, but we all know the mother earth is not real estate. It cannot be bought and sold. It is eternal. It is not to be fenced off. It is not to be desecrated by the foul machinery of capitalism. The gross obscenity for profit knows no bounds."

He was in deep thought, falling silent as the crowd waited for his next words. He continued. "You are slaves and don't even realize it. The privileged class uses their media empires to spread propaganda telling you how wonderful America is and how lucky you are to live here. They have stolen your elections by making sure a person of integrity is never a candidate, always offering a choice between the lesser of two evils. They have suppressed your will to fight. I tell you I am Jesus come with a mighty sword of retribution."

WHEN JESUS CAME TO THE BLACK HILLS
TO DO THE GHOST DANCE
WITH THE SPIRIT OF SITTING BULL

Aaron had seen the immense power of this man to spellbound audiences, but he was still amazed at how he could arouse intense passion in a crowd. Son of God? No! Aaron could not believe that, but son of anarchy, yes, he certainly was that.

Leland Abercrombie was on the phone with the President almost immediately after Aaron left. He supported the President not because he saw him as the best man for the job, but rather, as the best man to put more money in his family's pockets. In fact, he looked upon the President as a moron who would have never accomplished anything had he not inherited a fortune from his father. This was the way of America. You got ahead based upon the accomplishments of your relatives, not on your own merits. No matter what the industry, nepotism reigned supreme.

The President laughed the whole matter off, saying to Abercrombie, "This guy is a joke. What can the Injuns do? We are about to put a pipeline though the reservation, and they come up with a false messiah. These fools should go to Alabama or Mississippi, where I hoodwinked the backward buffoons into voting for me because they think I love Jesus more than my opponent and would protect their right to walk around Wal-Mart with AK-47's. The Injuns are almost as simple-minded as those southern crackers still fighting the Civil War and waving the confederate flag."

WHEN JESUS CAME TO THE BLACK HILLS
TO DO THE GHOST DANCE
WITH THE SPIRIT OF SITTING BULL

"But Mr. President," replied Abercrombie, "I think you should have the F.B.I. check things out. This guy Aaron Adam's has caused the U.S. government some problems in the recent past. He is not someone to be taken lightly I am afraid."

In his usual arrogant, cocky tone, the President replied, "I am the President. I fear no man and no country, and certainly not some rogue private eye hanging around with an idiot calling himself Jesus. I am the Jesus in this nation, and I'll have this Adams and fake Jesus nailed to a cross at the top of Mount Rushmore if they mess with me. You concentrate on getting that pipeline through. That is all you have to worry about."

The President hung up on Abercrombie who took a deep breath as he whispered to himself, "Still a goddamn moron, but a useful moron for rich people like me."

Walking through a land filled with pain,
Sometimes I think the world is insane.
What can I do but sing that old song
That says many have nothing to call their own.
Gazing at those who are on the outside looking in
Makes me realize greed I cannot defend.
Rolling through a land that makes a bend,
Will the institutionalized poverty ever end?
What a horrible puzzle a nation must face,
When compassion in its heart has no place.

WHEN JESUS CAME TO THE BLACK HILLS
TO DO THE GHOST DANCE
WITH THE SPIRIT OF SITTING BULL

The blue bird of happiness flies high above,
Unable to light when push comes to shove.
Time to wonder. Time to wonder.
Now the land is thrown asunder.
Will sanity of hope ever prevail,
So that compassion won't fail,
While the privileged are allowed to plunder.
Time to wonder. Time to wonder.

The author of this book served in the United States military during an abomination known as the Vietnam War. I have been under fire without much fighting as there are different types of battle, and spending most of my time in service at the Pentagon, where I saw the nefarious means used to subjugate and destroy those who dared stand against the tyranny of the American economic juggernaut made me aware of how the uneducated and poor are used as cannon fodder by an evil system that indoctrinates the youth of America with patriotic babble so they can serve the interests of the capitalists.

I often hang my head in shame to realize that through no fault of my own (there was a draft in those days) I contributed to an illegal and immoral war effort conducted in the name of freedom but, in reality, was nothing more than an abject criminal enterprise to protect the moneyed interests that were fearful of losing power and influence in a backwards Southeast Asian nation that simply wanted its freedom from American economic slavery. Thankfully, right actually won and the USA was soundly defeated militarily, but in the end, the very nation that fought against capitalistic exploitation is now embracing capitalism, so all the blood shed on both sides was for naught, because in the end greed seems to always win.

The coming war this time had the same elements, as a sovereign nation (The Lakota) was about to go up against the mighty U.S. government and its vaunted military machine that was every bit as ruthless as the German army that used blitzkrieg to subdue and subjugate all that dared stand in its way at the start of World War II.

America lost any moral authority it ever had in Vietnam, Afghanistan and Iraq. Its use of terrorism to fight terrorism finally laid bare its complete lack of any moral superiority in a world that saw the base hypocrisy that made it a pariah among nations that respected the rule of law. Understanding this lack of a moral core, Jesus had long ago planted the seeds of a rebellion that were growing into a crop of dedicated fighters willing to die in a stand against injustice. To comprehend how things got to this point, we must go back in time when Jesus was assumed to have been killed in Canada's Broughton Archipelago as an extremely Conservative Party Canadian Prime

WHEN JESUS CAME TO THE BLACK HILLS
TO DO THE GHOST DANCE
WITH THE SPIRIT OF SITTING BULL

Minister gave American troops the go-ahead to invade a First Nation's Reserve and subdue a rebellion led by a rebel-rouser calling himself Jesus.

Aaron Adams had been by his side and seen him crucified by a sadistic American general who slaughtered thousands while putting down a rebellion that the USA feared might spread to its shores. The crucifixion was to serve as a warning to anyone who might try to declare themselves sanctified and seek justice for natives.

Aaron barely escaped with his life and for five years assumed that his friend Jesus had died, but, in truth, his dead body was removed from the cross, placed on a military plane three days later and prepared for return to the USA, where it was decided he would be cremated and his ashes scattered at sea. The only problem was that before the plane took off, when the general came to inspect the cargo hold that housed his body, the body bag was empty and there was residual radioactivity discovered on the shroud in which he had been wrapped. The four men guarding the body were brutally interrogated, and accused of complacency in arranging for his body to be spirited away. The truth was stranger than fiction. They simply said that the slab on which the shrouded body was placed had never left the guarded plane. The lock was on the door when the general arrived, and none of the guards had been trusted with the key. How then did he get out and why the radiation?

It is not within the purview of this writer to answer that particular question, because no explanation is available, except for those who might believe this man actually is the real Jesus and can perform miracles. Was he resurrected as he claims to have been several times in several different places over two thousand years? Does it really matter? Is it actually germane to what I am recounting here? I believe it is not, and for that reason will simply move on with this incredibly remarkable story.

However, as alluded to earlier, in order to better understand what was about to occur at Wounded Knee, South Dakota we must go back to this time between the disappearance of Jesus' body and his dramatic arrival in the sacred Black Hills, because shortly after his aforementioned assumed resurrection, intricate plans for the ultimate showdown with the United States government were being formulated by Jesus. As with everything done by this extraordinary man, carefully meticulous planning was instituted with no consideration for how long it would take. For Jesus, according to his own pronouncements, was a man who was not constrained by time as we mere mortals are.

WHEN JESUS CAME TO THE BLACK HILLS
TO DO THE GHOST DANCE
WITH THE SPIRIT OF SITTING BULL

He never revealed how he managed to survive and escape from those who supposedly killed him, but survive he did, and he went into hiding in a small Canadian Sioux First Nations reservation in Saskatchewan known as White Bear Reserve. It was there, among the approximately 2000 Assiniboine Sioux, that he formulated his idea to help the great Sioux Nation rise up in unison against their American oppressors, which he believed would, in turn, make other tribes join in an assault against the racist policies of a nation that had practiced history's worst genocide against these noble people and systematically tried to erase them from existence. The Canadian government had only recently admitted to its genocidal policies, and under new leadership was trying to make amends – but not the USA.

The border between Canada and the USA around the reserve near Carlyle, Saskatchewan was convenient for ease of crossing at the Northgate Border Station between North Dakota and Saskatchewan, which was very lackadaisically manned by both countries. It was from the White Bear Reserve that Jesus managed to get word of his plans for a rebellion of the American Lakota to a group of sympathetic former military men. These men and a few women, who had fought in Afghanistan and Iraq, became disillusioned with American warmongering and the hypocritical use of its military, not to bring freedom to other nations, but to enslave them to the culture of greed that was spreading across the world like a plague, aided and abetted by the American military machine of oppression.

These people would be called traitors by the flag-waving masses, but were, in fact, true heroes in a nation that had long ago seen real freedom flow into a river of propagandized mediocrity where patriotism was measured by flag waving and shouts of "hallelujah" rather than true dedication to the ideals of democracy. In a nation where a man taking a knee while the National Anthem was played to protest racism was called a disrespectful cretin, but policemen who brutalized protestors and people of colour were hailed as heroes, it was little wonder that the few Americans still capable of reflective, analytical thought could see the hypocrisy that was crushing a nation that had simply lost its way.

Thus, on the White Bear reserve, a steady stream of freedom fighters made their way to see Jesus and discuss plans for a coming rebellion of the Lakota people that would shake the foundations of a nation that had no idea what real freedom was. It had become a nation where nearly half of the population was effectively brainwashed and conditioned by propaganda to believe the world was out to get them, when all the world really wanted was to be left alone to decide their own fates, unencumbered by the fake democracy promulgated by the world's biggest terrorist nation, a nation where the light of compassion has been dimmed so low that there is no way the path to hope can be seen.

It was at White Bear that Jesus clandestinely summoned Colonel Barton, who was known as a proponent of curtailing the U.S. military and its use as an instrument to subvert democratic movements all over the world. There, Jesus said to him, "You are a man of honour I believe, and for that reason I must ask you a very simple question. Would you be willing, as a patriot, to stand against your own government to support a people that it is suppressing in a concentration camp of misery called a reservation?"

Looking at him with sincerity, Barton replied, "I, and many of the men who served with me, have concluded that we served an abominable power bent on world domination by an economic order that will allow no dissent against the culture of greed. We have grown so weary that there are now thousands of us training for what we believe will be the inevitable battle to rescue America from the capitalistic fascists that have slowly eroded what little democracy is left. Would I stand against my own government? Yes, because when a government becomes intolerable, the tradition of patriots, honoured with blood, is rebellion."

WHEN JESUS CAME TO THE BLACK HILLS
TO DO THE GHOST DANCE
WITH THE SPIRIT OF SITTING BULL

Jesus then asked, "And what of the Native Americans? Would you stand with them against the power that has usurped moral authority and turned it against those who were here first to make them strangers in their own land, locked them in concentration camps they call by the more benign term of reservations and refuse to honour the treaties they signed guaranteeing them sovereignty over their homelands?"

"The treatment of Native Americans and the genocide practiced against them is much more abhorrent that what the Nazis did to the Jews in World War II. Standing with them would be an honour."

"Then Colonel, we need to start planning for a brand new American Revolution on the Sioux Reservations that will rock the foundations of a nation that has no moral core left. Join me and let us assemble a mighty army of hope with those who are willing to die for the cause of freedom and formulate a grand plan to bring justice to those who have been denied it for hundreds of years. We shall be fighting a formable foe, but like Joshua, who brought down the walls of Jericho, we will bring down the walls of hopelessness erected by the barons of greed and pound those who have no heart or soul into rubble before the might of a righteous army, whose chief weapon is justice."

WHEN JESUS CAME TO THE BLACK HILLS
TO DO THE GHOST DANCE
WITH THE SPIRIT OF SITTING BULL

From that day on, very slowly and methodically, Colonel Barton had his small army cross the border, and they began a five year training regimen until they grew into an army of thousands ready to follow Jesus into battle alongside the mighty warriors of the Sioux Nation, which were now undergoing training from the men who had slipped from Canada into Pine Ridge. However, this was not the only method they were undertaking to secure justice. To comprehend just how methodical and detailed Jesus' plan was, one must first understand the nature of America's nuclear weapons stockpile and the missiles they set atop. The missile silos where these weapons are or were is no secret. One can actually Google a map of them.

Many of the missiles and their command bunkers have been in the same place for decades. They are near county and state roads that offer public access to people. You need security clearances to access the actual active silo sites; but just as farmers plough the fields where some of the silos are located, the public drives by the sites without realizing the terrible destructive power within eyesight of the ones still operational. You simply cannot hide these from either the public or an adversary. This pantheon of destruction directed by a series of thunder bolt wielding autocrats in Washington suggested a patriarchy and the valuing of warrior skills over the pursuit of peace. America had the largest nuclear arsenal in the world, but hypocritically believed it had the moral authority to deny other nations the right to develop these weapons. As the only nation to ever use these horrendous weapons, in the two biggest terrorist attacks in history on civilians in the Japanese cities of Hiroshima and Nagasaki, it had no claim to the moral high ground it self-righteously staked out.

Many of the non-operational silos where these missiles had been stored now stood empty, most having been filled with concrete. However, a few had not been filled and in two something was happening that would serve as an ace-in-the hole for the Sioux Nation in its coming battle against the U.S. government, because deep within the two silos on the North Dakota-South Dakota border farm of Robert "Soaring Eagle" McLain was a terror that a group of dedicated patriots were prepared to unleash if defeat was imminent, a terror so devastating that nothing could stand before it without total annihilation. Colonel Barton, in consultation with Jesus, had made these two silos that had been built by the U.S. government to withstand a direct nuclear hit a strategic asset of the Sioux Army that was about to rise up against the nation that had subjugated it for hundreds of years. Now deserted as a result of the Strategic Arms Limitation Treaty that had reduced the number of ICBM's from enough to destroy the world twenty times over to being able to destroy it 10 times over, two silos were forgotten as they supposedly set empty. However, deep within these silos was a cadre of men working day and night for four years assembling weapons of mass destruction the likes of which no one could comprehend. Their use was reserved as a last resort, and later this author will detail its destructive power which was the result of the work of Dr. Myron Morrison, a person of assumed principle who had joined with Jesus to right the great wrong promulgated against the Sioux Nation and other Native American tribes that were victims of the world's greatest holocaust.

Barton said to Jesus when at White Bear Reserve, "I am tired of U.S. self-righteous hypocrisy."

Jesus grinned and replied, "Woe to you, teachers of the law and Pharisees, you hypocrites! You clean the outside of the cup and dish, but inside they are full of greed and self-indulgence. Blind Pharisee! First clean the inside of the cup and dish, and then the outside will also be clean."

Colonel Barton sighed and replied, "I have read that in the Bible. You quote it well."

"I, my friend, have said it thousands of times over thousands of years."

WHEN JESUS CAME TO THE BLACK HILLS
TO DO THE GHOST DANCE
WITH THE SPIRIT OF SITTING BULL

Again, the Colonel sighed and said, "I am throwing in with you, not because I believe you are some modern messiah, but because I believe in your powers of persuasion, your power to rouse people to action. What you did in New Jersey and the Broughton Archipelago may have ended in defeat for righteousness, but those two incidents proved to me your power of persuasion. Americans are the most complacent people on earth. They accept their fate, because their will to fight has been cut from their hearts and tossed into a scrap heap of lost hope. You give them hope, and the people who need the most hope in this nation are the Native Americans who have suffered the wrath of an abominable nation that uses religion and flag waving to enslave people to an idea of moral superiority that is as bankrupt as the millionaires who run the government."

Long ago, I said, "Do not assume that I come to bring peace to the earth. I have not come to bring peace but a sword."

"I have seen the sword used by this nation to subjugate and destroy all that dare stand against it. I was an instrument of this evil, and I want peace, not a sword, but I know that you cannot defeat these greed driven, arrogant bastards by pleading for justice. You must demand it. I stand with my sword ready to do your bidding and bring the Sioux Nation its dignity that was stolen so long ago, and hopefully many others in America will see their courage and stand with them against the evil barons of greed who have no heart or soul and only want more and more to satisfy their insatiable greed."

Jesus stood, walked to Barton, placed his hand on his shoulder and earnestly said, "This is a crusade that may fail as so many of my crusades have, but these noble people will fail on their feet, not on their knees. Let us prepare for the coming battle."

They were atop a mesa on the plains of Saskatchewan. It was here that Sitting Bull had come to escape the wrath of the U.S. Army after he defeated Custer at Little Big Horn, the last great victory of the Sioux Nation against the U.S. Army. Jesus pointed upward and lightning pierced the dark skies as thunder clamoured in a cascading rolling symphony of indignation as the natives and Barton's men at the base of the mesa stood in awe of Jesus, the man who had roused in them a commitment to exact retribution for all the wrongs suffered by these noble people. In the middle of the sky, the clouds parted and a bright light penetrated between the clouds. There, riding on painted horses, two men – one a fierce, muscular-laden, broad shouldered warrior with a prominent nose who sat astride the animal carrying him bouncing up and down with a determination that spoke of a coming storm of indignation that would light the fires of hell against any who dared stand in the way of justice. The other was a meek looking, scholarly chief with a flowing war bonnet that hung to the flanks of the horse upon which he rode. The natives in the throng began to shout, "Crazy Horse and Sitting Bull," as the military men among them gasped in awe at what they were witnessing. It was here, among the Canadian Sioux, that Jesus was beginning to build his army, and these Sioux, along with Barton's men would cross the border and prepare to unleash the coming Armageddon on the U.S. government.

The clouds converged, the two mighty warriors disappearing into darkness. As one giant bolt of thunder lit up the sky.

Jesus then shouted to those below "I am raising up an end time army that is strong and courageous. You are all part of that army. I demand men and women of valour - bold, strong and defiant in battle. As you stand immovable and refuse to be intimidated, I will cause your enemies who rise up against you to be defeated before you; and they will come out against you one way and will flee before you. I am calling forth the warriors of old who will never retreat when the adversary comes against them, because I have anointed their hands for war and their fingers for battle. Those whom I place on the front lines are those who are able to stand against the evil of a hypocritical nation that has no compassion, no heart and no soul. We are about to embark on a righteous crusade against the most potent military on earth, a military with brainwashed soldiers who believe they are somehow always on the right side, but are, in reality serving masters of deceit. Their house of cards is about to tumble before a mighty wind of retribution. Prepare my brethren for the battle of Armageddon."

Jesus was arousing them now, as he continued, "My warriors will recognize that it is not flesh and blood that they are battling against but the powers of darkness and wickedness driven by greed. You must all have the fierceness of lions. Our evil enemies must see the tenacity inside of you; therefore, they will cower in fear before you. We go against a kingdom of darkness and must stand immovable in the face of adversity. We must be as swift as gazelles on the mountains, mobile, active men and women; ready to fight wherever and whenever the need arises. I shall go to the Black Hills and arouse a sleeping giant there as you prepare to join us in the great battle against the Satanic forces that have commandeered a nation and systematically fomented a culture of self-righteousness and greed that spreads its evil across the world like an ancient plague. We are the doctors who are about to cure this disease, about to stop its spread with a mighty dose of medicine that has been incubated in the laboratory of freedom. Our drug is a big dose of justice!"

CHAPTER 7
WE SHALL PREVAIL IN THE END

"These *people I lead to glory,*
All heroes of an unwritten story.
They all born of a mighty mother,
Hope rests in their hearts with one another.
They now rise, like lions after slumber,
In unvanquishable, uncontrollable number.
They shake their chains to earth like dew,
Which will eventually strangle and crush you."

"What is Freedom? Natives can easily tell,
For they have known slavery all too well.
Today, in every native, courage has grown
To an echo of their destiny to finally own.
You can hear them clear and loud.

J. Wayne Frye   149

WHEN JESUS CAME TO THE BLACK HILLS
TO DO THE GHOST DANCE
WITH THE SPIRIT OF SITTING BULL

You kept my people in a dark cell,
While tyrants in high places did dwell."

"Leonard Peltier lies in a cell you made.
But justice he can still plough and spade;
With or without your own will, he did not bend
Before the evil cretins you did send.
You wanted to make native children weak,
So of injustice they might not speak.
But now the winter winds are forming,
And new warriors will soon be swarming."

Men are ordinarily governed by their habits or deluded by their wishes. Most, led by the phantoms of deception, and ambitious for that ever elusive affluence, seek the mines of gold offered in a system of greed; but by far, the greater portion of the humankind must be content with crumbs from the tables of plenty set for the few. Most see the empty empire of greed and accept their fate as slaves to a system that preys on the non-rich to serve the needs of the affluent.

Thus, Aaron and Mary observed the Black Hills ministry of Jesus, not to bring peace, but to sow anarchy, for only through violent upheaval had any great accomplishment in social justice ever been achieved. As they stood watching Jesus preach at the very spot where the images of Sitting Bull and Crazy Horse, just at they had done in Saskatchewan, appeared at the cave entrance, they wondered how many spies from Washington were among the crowd, and how long it would take for the government to act against these conspirators.

As they pondered diligently on this, the words of this son of anarchy reverberated all about, sending cold shivers up and down the spines of those gathered there. "I tell you that here today there are those among us who are despicable spies in service to injustice. Look at the one standing beside you, and let him know that no amount of spies, no underhanded slimy creature representing the moneyed class will ever deter you. In fact, urge him or her to free themselves and embrace real freedom with us as we engage in the gloriously righteous pursuit of justice. He who cannot protect himself or his nearest and dearest or their honour by non-violently facing death may and ought to do so by violently dealing with the oppressor. He who can do neither of the two is a burden. He has no business to be the head of a family. He must either hide himself, or must rest content to live forever in helplessness and be prepared to crawl like a worm at the bidding of a bully in the Washington White House that serves the affluent. When violence is offered in self-defence or for the defence of the defenceless, it is an act of bravery far better than cowardly submission. Even Ghandi believed that violence was justified when all else failed."

WHEN JESUS CAME TO THE BLACK HILLS
TO DO THE GHOST DANCE
WITH THE SPIRIT OF SITTING BULL

"Remember that it was not the peaceful demonstrations of Martin Luther King that secured the civil rights of the African Americans. Rather, it was the anarchists shouting burn baby burn as they put torches to the ghettos that were concentration camps of despair. These acts of anarchy struck fear in the hearts of the white people that their neighbourhoods might be next and motivated those in power to throw the people of colour a bone. That bone has never been thrown to Native Americans, and we will not accept a bone, even if it is thrown, as it was to the African-Americans. For we do not seek a token acknowledgement of justice, but we demand complete, irrevocable justice born from the screams of our hungry, our forgotten, our oppressed who will rain anarchy upon the oppressor until we stand triumphant on the mountain of hope."

At a little distance in front of the crowd upon a knoll stood Aaron, who, by his position and air, appeared to stand out. He was tall, somewhat muscular, way past middle age with greying hair, of a dull countenance and displayed a listless manner that made one realize this was not a man with whom one should trifle. His frame appeared loose and flexible; but it was vast, and in reality of prodigious power. There was a latent aura that seemed to shine about him like the slumbering and unwieldy, but terrible, strength of the elephant.

WHEN JESUS CAME TO THE BLACK HILLS
TO DO THE GHOST DANCE
WITH THE SPIRIT OF SITTING BULL

The interior lineaments of his countenance were coarse, extended and vacant; while the superior, or those nobler parts which are thought to affect the intellectual being, were low, receding and lean looking. He was a man who exuded confidence borne of necessity in his world where he had to deal with the seedy side of humankind to earn his living as a private detective. Mary stood in admiration of the man she had grown to love as the sun fell below the crest of the majestic Black Hills, while Jesus concluded his remarks and the crowd, most carrying weapons, dispersed, prepared now to do battle for justice when called upon by this son of anarchy. In the centre of this sudden flood of fiery light dancing about the scared hills, stood Aaron Adams to whom was drawn Jesus. With Colonel Barton by his side, Jesus seemed a smaller man than he was, but there was something in his stride, his countenance that made him appear colossal in purpose; his attitude musing and intensely serious.

The effect of such a spectacle was instantaneous and powerful. The man in front of Aaron stood smiling at him while his long, scraggily chestnut hair blew slightly in the evening breeze. He turned to Mary and said about Aaron, "Like me, you are growing to love this man, because you see that despite his often abrupt and direct manner, his intolerance for stupidity and his penchant for directness with profane language, he is a man who hates injustice and extends the hand of compassion to those who live in the squalor caused by capitalism."

Still looking at Mary, he continued. "He does not believe in God, nor does he believe in me. This man with no religion has more religion than anyone I have ever known, for he lives with a fierce devotion to justice, which is real religion. He sees the folly of fairy tales, but believes in the words of Jesus that preach of hope and peace, but he knows that the only way to achieve peace and justice is by the sword, not the meek pleading for justice from those who do not know the meaning of the word. He dances in the sunlight of hope, not hypocrisy. He waltzes with the queen of disorder and hostility in the halls of power where he shines the light of retribution upon those who have hijacked the country and instituted the culture of greed. He is my strong right hand in the coming of Armageddon. He will shake his head in disgust at what I say, but he sees within me hope for a nation that has always worshipped at the altar of avarice disregard for common decency."

Aaron, shaking his head, said, "You're full of rhetorical bullshit."

Putting his arm around Aaron, Jesus led him, Barton and Mary toward a limousine with the motor idling that was waiting nearby. He reached down, opened the door and said, "Get in. We have an emissary from the White House; a representative of that bombastic buffoon far too many people believed would resurrect the glory of this lost nation."

Lu Ann Luce was an advisor to the President, a woman who would sell her soul for 30 pieces of silver. Her only real allegiance was to herself and to the aggrandizement she sought, like her boss, to puff up her ego.

Jesus, got into the car and sat in the jump seat. In an extremely polite manner, he introduced himself and his three friends. Then, without hesitation or equivocation, he said, "So, tell me what you offer from that buffoon who fancies himself a leader."

"I am here to meet with you, not with these people. First, you must have them leave immediately, and must also change your tone if we are to make progress on negotiations to bring an end to this folly."

"First, these people are my compatriots, and I shall discuss nothing without them present. Second, do not ask me to show respect for that idiot you serve for your own selfish reasons who got everything he has, because he was born with a silver spoon in his mouth. I show respect to those who earn it, not those who think they were born into it. Now, what do you have to offer? My time is valuable."

"If you end this ridiculous talk of rebellion immediately, we are prepared to offer you safe conduct out of this country and a nice stipend for life. The alternative you do not want to know, because you are dealing with a President who acts like a President."

Tis to hunger for such diet,
As the rich man in his riot
Casts to the poor dogs that lie
Surfeiting beneath his eye.

Jesus eased back in the jump seat, pointed over at Mary and said to Luce, "This is a woman who has prostituted herself. She sold herself to men and maybe even women for a price, but she was never a hypocrite about it. She made a living by bringing pleasure and never hid that fact. You prostitute yourself every day before the altar of greed in service to a man with no moral core. This woman is virtuous in her heart, because within her beats compassion for the downtrodden. You, however, are an abomination, because you prostitute yourself to a man of low character for your own welfare. You lie day in and day out in defence of the defenceless. Go back to your boss in Washington, or at one of the golf clubs where he spends most of his time and tell him that the son-of-man is not for sale. Unlike him, I do not come with a price tag. Tell him that like he did during the Viet Nam War, he had better hide from the coming battle and send out his lackeys to die for his lies while he cowers in fear. We will accept no compromise. The treaties entered into by the U.S. government with the Lakota Nation must be reaffirmed, the pipelines shut off, all government offices on Lakota land closed, and reparations negotiations earnestly entered into to compensate the people for years of abuse. We are all prepared to die for this cause, and when you send the fascist military machine onto this scared land, tell the soldiers that they will face annihilation of the most brutal kind."

Arrogantly, she replied, "You think you can stand against the U.S. Military?"

"The monumental buffoon you serve will probably order an aircraft carrier into the Black Hills. He is the biggest moron to ever prop his feet up on the desk in the Oval Office. The ignorant will serve him, as they march to the waving flags of false patriotism and invoke the name of God in what they will be told is a righteous cause in defence of the liberty they don't even have. However, just as the ignorant who voted for him have gradually seen the error they made, the military will eventually turn against him and his culture of greed."

WHEN JESUS CAME TO THE BLACK HILLS
TO DO THE GHOST DANCE
WITH THE SPIRIT OF SITTING BULL

The anger was becoming palpable now in her contorting heavily make-upped encased face. She took a deep breath and said, "I will not be talked to that way."

Jesus, smiling and pointing to the door so everyone knew it was time to leave, said with compete disdain for the President's emissary, "Listen you self-righteous hypocritical bitch, I and those I serve will not be trifled with anymore. The Lakota people are off their knees and bow before no man or woman. Tell your fat-assed, arrogant, egotistical boss in that inglorious house of hypocrisy on the Potomac that his day has come. He can give the Lakota what is rightfully theirs, or we'll burn the White House to the ground like the Canadians did in 1814 with, as he enjoys saying, a fire and fury like the world has never seen."

Despite the constant contrary propaganda, nobleness in the treatment of Native Americans or any other groups of people they wanted to subjugate has never been a trait practiced by the United States military, and as the four left the car, Lu Ann Luce was immediately on the phone, directing the band of Green Berets hiding nearby, who to a fair-minded observer, resembled demons rather than men, sporting their arrogantly crooked berets, were approaching the four as they briskly walked back to a waiting car at a fearful rate. Aaron and Colonel Barton were frantically urging

Jesus and Mary onward, sensing they were being tracked.

At intervals, the slight rustling of silenced booted feet was borne along by the night wind, quite audibly in their front and rear, and their progress through the rising fog was swift and measured; adding to the unearthly appearance of the spectacle. They would be sitting ducks in the car, so Barton and Aaron pushed Jesus and Mary behind a nearby trash dumpster as they crouched down and put their index fingers to their lips to indicate silence should be maintained.

Aaron and Barton, veterans of war, used watchful eyes and keen ears to assess the band behind and in front of them. Barton signalled with his right hand flashing five, five and then two, indicating that there were 12 men after them.

Barton and Aaron had their revolvers out as the two separate bands edged towards the stream near them. Happily, for the hidden party, the extremely tall grass around them acted as additional concealment. Aaron and Barton crawled through the tall grass and peered at the two bands as they came together on the banks of the stream. At length an athletic looking brawny man, obviously by his air of authority, seemingly the leader, summoned the others about him for consultation. This body of evil was collected on the very margin of that mass of tall grass in which the party of four were hidden. The smallest motion would be sure to bring these cautious soldiers rushing toward them. Their caution indicated superior military training, where no move would be made until success was almost 100% guaranteed. Barton had counted twelve of them, but only eight were by the river.

They were about to return to the two by the dumpster, when a rustle to their left signalled an alert. To their surprise, four men stood above them with M-4 rifles cocked and ready to terminate them if they made a wrong move. Notwithstanding the surprise and the disadvantage they faced, the two dropped their pistols on the ground as one of the men picked them up without uttering a word. Quicker than a flash, the whole party of soldiers from the river area surrounded them and walked them back toward the dumpster where Jesus and Mary were compelled to yield themselves as prisoners also. The four had been dishonourably set-up by Lu Ann Luce.

Notwithstanding the peaceable submission of the four, they were all quite aware of the character of the band into whose hands they had unceremoniously fallen. The Green Berets had no sooner deprived the captives of their weapons that they took on an air of invincibility and arrogance, forcibly pulling and shoving the four about, and as is customary for an army that enjoys instilling fear, they hooded them as a further element of intimidation.

Although the four could no longer see what was going on, it was obvious that they were going to be spirited off the reservation and probably locked up in a nearby military facility. Slowly and deliberately, they were being urged forward over what was familiar ground to Mary. They were near the stream bank and headed toward a soccer field at the Park of Native Martyrs, where, no doubt, a helicopter would pick them up.

Most of the group's dark forms blended with the brown of the prairie. The hooded captives were unable to discern a human figure, but they could still, with keen listening, sense a moving, and constantly increasing circle, as conjecture and added apprehension were overwhelming them.

In this manner passed many anxious and weary minutes, during the close of which the listeners expected at each moment to hear the whirring rotor blades of a helicopter. However, at the expiration of half an hour, the four began to appear gloomy and sullen, as the gravity of the situation took hold.

"Our time is at hand," observed Jesus, who noted the smallest incident, or the slightest indication of hostility among their captors. "They have been told to interrogate us. It is dark, and they want to wait until dawn to extract us. Am I right Colonel Barton?"

"Yes, strategically, a day time extraction would be better."

The soldiers suddenly jerked the bags from their faces and the sergeant in charge stood arrogantly before the four. "Shut up you treasonous dogs. You are dealing with the U.S. Army now."

Colonel Barton said, "You are a fucking disgrace to the name U.S. Army, serving that fat-assed mini-Mussolini who struts around like Napoleon. If you were real men, you would join us in the fight against injustice promulgated against the Lakota Nation, the fight against poverty, the fight against greed, the fight against patriotic propaganda that is imprisoning all of you in service to a despot."

The burly but buff sergeant quickly raised his right foot and slammed it hard into the colonel's mid-section, shoving him onto his back, placed his foot on his chest and said, "I'll snuff out your life you traitorous bastard. Shut the fuck up."

"Do it asshole. Go ahead, pull the damn trigger. That is all you are good for. You stopped thinking for yourself long ago, stopped believing in any duty but to the moneyed class that rules your life. The moneyed class that you serve like the slave you are. Pull the goddamn trigger you fucking excuse of a human being."

Jesus very calmly interjected, "You pull that trigger and you do not slay him. You slay any hope you have of salvation as a human being. The people you serve have not only captured your body to serve the interests of the moneyed class, but they have captured your mind and soul, made you a consumer of their flag-waving, fake Jesus-loving patriotic propaganda that has turned your mind into mush, made you an instrument of repression the world over in service to a bankrupt idea of superiority. Do the right thing and join me, the son-of-man, who is here to provide you with a map to real freedom, a map to the glory of justice. Make a decision to stop serving those who look upon you with disdain and only honour your service when it serves their selfish interests."

"We have been warned about your powers of persuasion with rhetorical skills that spout out communist propaganda that is used to destroy our way of life."

Smiling, Jesus replied, "Your way of life? Here you are risking that very life for a few thousand dollars a month. Meanwhile the generals who order you into battle sit safely behind the lines and make five times what you do, and when they are through ordering you to serve their moneyed masters they will be put on the boards of corporations while you are given a measly stipend that will never buy you a ticket on the train of prosperity. You will cynically be thanked for your service by thoroughly programmed patriots every bit as ignorant as you are. You simply line up for the chains and manacles that will imprison you the rest of your life to those who make a mockery of economic and social justice."

In the meantime, a small cadre of Colonel Barton's men and a few Lakota warriors had not been idle, as word of what happened had filtered to them through the observations of a group of youngsters who had seen the group being captured. Profiting by the high fog, which grew in the area, they had wormed their way through the matted grass until the point was gained where an extraordinary caution became necessary to their further advance. Bartholomew Soaring Eagle, keen observer, had occasionally elevated his dark, grim countenance above the herbage, straining his eyeballs to penetrate the gloom that skirted the border of the field where his four compatriots were held. Along with Colonel Barton's aide, Hiram Holiday, in these momentary glances, he gained sufficient knowledge to be master of the position staked out by the Green Berets.

WHEN JESUS CAME TO THE BLACK HILLS
TO DO THE GHOST DANCE
WITH THE SPIRIT OF SITTING BULL

They were somewhat baffled by the stillness of the camp, which lay in a quiet as deep as if it were literally a place of the dead. Too wary and distrustful to rely, in circumstances of so much doubt, on the discretion of any less firm and crafty than themselves, they bade their companions remain where they lay and pursued the reconnoitring alone.

The progress of the two was now extremely slow and painfully laborious. However, the methodical advance of the wily ones was noiseless and determined. They drew steadily foot by foot through the tall bending grass, pausing at each movement to catch the smallest sound that might betray any knowledge on the part of the Green Berets of their proximity. They succeeded, at length, in dragging themselves out of the sickly light of the full moon, into the dark shadows of the field, where the surrounding objects became more distinctly visible to their keen and active glances. Here, they paused long and warily to observe before venturing any further. Their position enabled them to bring the whole encampment into a dark but clearly marked profile; furnishing a distinct clue by which the newly minted warriors were led to a tolerably accurate estimate of the force they were about to encounter. Still, an unnatural silence pervaded the spot, as they signalled for their men to now edge their way forward toward them.

J. Wayne Frye   165

WHEN JESUS CAME TO THE BLACK HILLS
TO DO THE GHOST DANCE
WITH THE SPIRIT OF SITTING BULL

Men of nerves less tried than those of the fierce Bartholomew and Hiram would not have been so cautious, but knowing the reputation of Green Berets for cunningness, they were surprised at how lackadaisical they were about guarding the perimeters of the encampment. Obviously, they assumed the natives and their allies were not to be taken seriously as warriors.

When certain that they were undiscovered, Hiram slowly crawled within two feet of the lone man guarding the approach to the field in that sort of wanton and subtle manner with which the reptile is seen to play about its victim before it strikes. Satisfied at length, not only of the slipshod professionalism but of the arrogant character of the stranger, Hiram seized the knife which hung at his side, and in an instant it was poised in his hand as he readied a charge. Then changing his purpose, with an action as rapid as his own flashing thoughts, he sunk back behind the trunk of the fallen tree against which Bartholomew waited, and lay in its shadow motionless.

The slothful sentinel scanned the quiet terrain, and gazing upward for a moment at the hazy heavens, he made an extraordinary exertion, and raised his powerful frame upright. Then he looked about him, with an air of something like watchfulness, suffering his dull glances to run over the misty open prairie beyond the playing field. Just at that moment, the twenty men with Hiram and Bartholomew methodically positioned themselves for an assault on the encampment.

Suddenly, in order to instil fear in those they were pursuing, the band of rescuers let out with shrieks, shouts and yells from mouths on every side of the Green Berets, indicating a force of greater number than was the reality. The guards still maintained their posts at the side of the captives, but it was with that sort of difficulty with which steeds are restrained at the starting-post, when expecting the signal to commence a wild and furious horse race. They held their fire as the shouts came from all about, and indicated more an opening parrying than a charge.

Hiram shouted out, "You are out-numbered 10 to 1, throw down your weapons."

The sergeant, putting his rifle to Barton's head, said, "I'll blow his goddamn brains out."

Hiram replied, just as he knew the Colonel would want. "Do it then, and we'll blow every last one of you bastards away. Go ahead, make your stupid play and die."

The sergeant's men all looked at him with fear in their eyes. He took a deep breath and whispered to Barton, "Tell him I mean business."

WHEN JESUS CAME TO THE BLACK HILLS
TO DO THE GHOST DANCE
WITH THE SPIRIT OF SITTING BULL

Barton smiled as he said, "Do it Hiram. Blow these bastards away if they do not drop their weapons at the count of five." He then began to count, "One, two."

"Wait, wait," the sergeant shouted, as doubts filtered into his patriotically brainwashed mind.

You have only had a taste of Anarchy
In your seat of power and malarkey,
But rest assured more is on the way,
For the Natives are about to have their day.

The typical white American is apt to boast that his or her nation may claim a descent more truly honourable than that of any other people. This is the norm in a nation that lacks those with the intellectual capacity to see the brainwashing propaganda that is constantly spewed out by those who manipulate the masses into serving the needs of the moneyed class. Even the original colonists, who are aggrandized as patriots who were in search of religious freedom were not looking for freedom from religion, but rather the freedom to impose their particular brand of religion, without equivocation, on others. Those who dared stray from the defined path of righteousness were put in stocks, shunned or even, in extreme cases, burned at the stake. The descendants of these simple and single-minded provincials stood there in their U.S. Army uniforms before the band of Sioux and

Colonel Barton's men. These Green Berets were the modern approbation of a superior attitude that left an unyielding core. The march of civilization had moved forward in the rest of the world, but the USA had always been restrained in progress by marriage to self-aggrandizing flag-waving and belief that somehow God had made Americans special.

The gradations of society, from that state which is called refined to that which approaches as near barbarity as connection with an intelligent people will readily allow, are to be traced from the bosom of the hypocrisy practiced by men who had the gall to put in a document that is revered by unthinking Americans that "all men were created equal," while the very signers of that declaration were slaveholders. There, on this darkest of nights, with these men, was the evolutionary process as a static manifestation of all that was wrong with a nation that represented the very worst of hypocrisy. The 12 white Green Berets had fallen for the hype that convinced them of their superiority, which they sincerely believed gave them the right to impose the will of America on the entire world.

Thus, these men faced a dilemma that they had never considered before. They could die for their air of superiority or they could lay down their weapons and submit.

WHEN JESUS CAME TO THE BLACK HILLS
TO DO THE GHOST DANCE
WITH THE SPIRIT OF SITTING BULL

Jesus, in his soft, but powerful voice said, "You men serve a power that has perverted the meaning of freedom. Put down your weapons. Do not die in vain for a man who sits on his throne of arrogance in the White House, a man who, himself, when he had the chance, avoided military service, because he was a hypocritical scion of privilege, a cowardly bombastic buffoon who would have never achieved anything without daddy's money and influence."

The sergeant took a deep breath and tossed down his weapon as he ordered the other men to do the same. Thus was avoided a certain blood bath. The Sioux and Barton's men had them remove their clothes. They put on the uniforms and prepared to commandeer the helicopters. The nearly naked men were marched off toward a deserted church at the place where the 1973 rebellion was sanctified.

The first battle had been fought with such finesse by the Lakota and their allies that bloodshed was thankfully avoided. However, Jesus, as those around him celebrated, said, "The coming battles will not be this easy, for we are up against a foe with formable power and a total belief in their cause, and they are superior in weapons and manpower, but remember we are superior in righteousness and we shall prevail in the end."

CHAPTER 8
THE FLICKERING EMBERS OF AGE

*Tis to let the ghost of gold
Take from toil a thousand fold,
More than any other substance could
As Natives in reverence never would.*

*Money is white man's God, but it is forged paper,
Which never opens the door to the great maker.
White man hoards something he thinks of worth,
When he needs just a hand full of Mother Earth.*

*He is but a slave in soul,
As money is in control.
Over his will it reins,
But Anarchy has no restraints.*

J. Wayne Frye   171

WHEN JESUS CAME TO THE BLACK HILLS
TO DO THE GHOST DANCE
WITH THE SPIRIT OF SITTING BULL

In Washington, D.C., the biggest buffoon to ever call himself President, who had just recently finished another one of his golf-excursions that along with watching television was his chief reason for getting up every morning, pounded his desk with his tiny little hands. His lack of vocabulary mastery was no different from any other time, as his third grade mentality was reflected in the words he used. "I don't understand what these Injuns want. We give the bums welfare so they don't have to work. I mean why don't they just stop pretending to be anything but what they are, a pack of leeches."

Calling the poor bums and welfare cheats is a bit disingenuous when it comes from a hypocrite who inherited his wealth from his father and would not last a day on a factory floor doing some real work. This President was a man who started out at the top and assumed everyone else was a loser, because they did not have his advantages. This is America at its worst, a place where the privileged never have to do an honest day's work, and never bend over to give someone a hand up. America did not have its royal leeches like the British and so many other countries with pampered royals who parade around like peacocks in full bloom, but the USA does have its own unique form of royalty. In America, royalty is based on the size of your bank account, and that bank account is usually passed on from one generation to another as an oligarchy has been in control for hundreds of years. And sitting behind that desk in the Oval Office was the apex of American royalty as the ignorant masses had actually elected this buffoon of privilege just as they had one of his predecessors, George W. Bush, another scion of privilege who never knew the meaning of work. The unwashed masses who elected these clowns are the same ones who must suffer the consequences of their folly. And what a folly it was with this bombastic, arrogant, narcissistic moron who had handed the keys to the kingdom over to corporations and the wealthy, the very ones who wanted the riches of the Black Hills.

One of his advisers said, in earnest, "Mr. President, we should try to make a deal with these people to avert any political fallout that might affect your re-election."

"Are you kidding, my brashness, my refusal to follow convention is what got me here. My people want a man-of-action, not a namby-pamby weakling who doesn't stand up to the people of colour who have been catered to for years. I will not allow anyone to question my authority. I am in control of this country. The people elected me to shake things up. If these Injuns fuck with me, I'll turn the white supremacists loose in the Black Hills, and see how they like that. My people will always back me 100%. They are too stupid to think for themselves. They let me do it for them. They are the ones who put me here, put me in control of a government that is here to promote capitalism, real capitalism for the people who really count, the people who are the engines of commerce that makes this nation great. The fucking poor who live in squalor are no longer a drag on this nation thanks to me. We have finally discarded them and let them rot in the slums where they prowl around like rats scurrying for a scrap of food, just as we will discard these damn Injuns who want to go back to a time when they worshipped what they call mother earth. Well, I call mother earth a resource that should be exploited, and these malcontents will not stand in the way of progress."

The President's somewhat scholarly looking chief-of-staff had tried unsuccessfully to rein in his penchant for brash actions in the past, but like Lu Ann Luce, he sacrificed any integrity he had when he agreed to serve this monumental idiot whose only goal in life was to seek out aggrandizement from those who served his narcissism. Daniel Ormond had no depth of character, had no self-respect, had no real soul as he bowed before a man of such low character. This was not a President; this was a self-promoting, arrogant, privileged, bullying snake that crawled about in the slime of his own making looking for the next victim to bite.

WHEN JESUS CAME TO THE BLACK HILLS
TO DO THE GHOST DANCE
WITH THE SPIRIT OF SITTING BULL

People who want to feel important promulgate most of the harm that is done in the world. They have no remorse for the evil they do as long as it gives them that sense of importance, and they justify it because they are absorbed in the endless struggle to think well of themselves. Deep down in their cancerous psyche that is rotting their souls they are desperate to think well of themselves, as subconsciously they realize just how shallow they are. Narcissists are great con artists as they succeed in deluding themselves. As a result, very few people see through them. In fact, many people admire them, which accounted for the current moron sitting in the Oval Office, as people actually fell for his con. This narcissism was about to lead to a battle between the power of good (Jesus) to confront evil (the President).

The President said to Ormond, "My loyal servant, Lu Ann Luce, is right now arranging for a squad of Green Berets to throttle this rebellion before it gets started. She will see that I get credit for stopping a rebellion before it gets started." Of course, he had no idea at the time what had occurred at Wounded Knee.

Though the encampment of Barton's men and the Lakota band contained many an eye that was long unclosed, and many an ear that listened greedily to catch the faintest evidence of any new alarm, they all lay in deep quiet during the remainder of the night. Silence and fatigue finally performed their accustomed offices, and before the morning, all but the sentinels were buried in sleep.

Just as day, however, began to dawn, and the sun was arching up on the horizon above the dusky objects of the plain, the half startled, anxious, and yet blooming countenance of Mary Morning Dove, who lay next to Aaron, was reared above the confused mass of warriors there as she heard off in the distance a faint sound, "whup-whup-whup-whup." It was a sound of horror for Aaron, as he jumped upright and stared blurry-eyed at Mary. For a second, thinking he was back in the rice patties of Vietnam, where his youth was squandered in an ill-fated adventure of conquest, he feared the sound as precursor to a blood bath as these whirring machines of destruction could rain down a torrent of searing fire upon the unsuspecting. He aroused those who had dressed in the Green Berets' uniforms and they all assembled in preparation to make their way to the two helicopters that had come to pick up the Green Berets and their captives. All there were ready now, ready to confront the immediate evil that had come to Wounded Knee.

Aaron, Mary, Barton and Jesus prepared to act as hostages as those dressed in the Green Beret uniforms surrounded them and moved out briskly toward the landing field where the choppers awaited. They hoped to capture the helicopters without bloodshed, but they knew that they were but poor relatively untrained soldiers in a battle against the well-armed and well-prepared merchants of death and mayhem who serve the wealthy. These recently minted native warriors were on a mission to raise the flag of victory against despots who used the military as an instrument against any who dared stand in defiance against the culture of greed. They were noble combatants ready to unleash mayhem against a nation that had trampled on decency and compassion as it paraded around the world with hypocritical arrogance steamrolling through country after country in defence of the indefensible. The pride soared in the people who had been on their knees far too long as they moved gingerly toward the helicopters.

The day fairly opened on the interminable waste of the undulating prairie. As the two choppers touched down, a door gunner from the rear of each aimed the M-60 death dealers they manned at the group moving forward toward the choppers. Hiram was leading one group and his lieutenant, Harlan Dobbs, the other. Unsuspecting, the gunners did nothing as the soldiers hopped aboard, but one man moved behind the gunners on each chopper and put a knife to their throats, causing instant panic.

WHEN JESUS CAME TO THE BLACK HILLS
TO DO THE GHOST DANCE
WITH THE SPIRIT OF SITTING BULL

Two soldiers, rifles in hands, moved toward the front where the pilots and co-pilots of both choppers were and said, "Cut your engine."

Thus, another smooth operation led to the bloodless commandeering of two choppers for the cause, as the pilots and the gunners were led to the compound and imprisoned with the others. Meanwhile, as Lu Ann Luce, after a night's rest, was making her way along U.S. Route 18 to the Deadwood Airport where a private jet awaited, she got a call. The man on the other end said, "This is Jesus, the men you sent to spirit us away to some torture hole are now our prisoners, and we also have the two choppers. Keep an eye above as you go toward Deadwood. We may decide to blow that limousine off the road, and if you make it back to that buffoon you serve, tell him we are ready to negotiate, and if not, we are ready for war."

Looking out the window skyward, her heart was racing rapidly as she said, "You don't have any idea what you are about to have rain down on the Lakota people. This President will not tolerate any disrespect."

"Lu Ann, tell that cretin whose boots you lick for personal gain that so far there has been no deaths, but we can change that in the blink of an eye if he makes the wrong move. This is not some reality TV show that he is starring in. This is reality in its purest form, not some loosely scripted mindless entry into mass culture that degrades everyone's intelligence and turns the public's brains into mush. We all can think, unlike the idiots who voted for him, falling for his lies like little children who believe in Santa Claus. You tell that golf-loving fat buffoon that we will take his golf cart away from him and drive it up his ass if he messes with us. Also, tell him we now have 18 hostages, and any move on our compound will result in their deaths – which will be his fault, not ours. The idiot is not playing with amateurs here. This is serious business and we are not afraid of him, his money or his power. End of conversation, and keep looking skyward, because we know how to rain down terror just as well as the military that serves your bombastic boss. Bye."

Aaron said, "Maybe we should really let those choppers buzz her just to scare her a bit."

Jesus smiled and nodded at Colonel Barton, who told his lieutenant to alert the two chopper pilots who were part of his squad to do as instructed in order to send a stern message.

As the men left, heading toward the choppers, they glanced back at the compound. In the bell tower of the abandoned church that the rebels had made their headquarters, nothing was visible that would be deemed a threat. The heavens were clothed in driving clouds; piled in vast masses one above the other. The wind whirled violently in occasional gusts; quieting occasionally, to admit transient glimpses of the bright and glorious sight of the heavens, dwelling in a magnificence by far too grand and durable to be disturbed by the fitful efforts of the lower world where now rebellion and the coming calamity hung mercilessly over all there. Beneath the bell tower, people were congregating in preparation for battle on the naked prairie of South Dakota. Amid the monotonous rolling of the landscape, a throng of thousands on the margin of the little church compound moved in hope for freedom, rifles on their shoulders and in their hands, as if each one was loaded with bullets that would sear the air with indignation for all the years they had suffered at the hands of oppressors.

Standing tall and defiant on the church steps, Jesus greeted the throng. His voice, calm and measured, reached their hearts with words that aroused them to vow no retreat from the new pride that they had found. He said, "I have journeyed from a failed rebellion five years ago to this spot now, determined to never fail again in rousing people to get off their knees. Neither you nor I will ever be better than we are right at this moment, a moment when we all here reach out with love for one another and determination not to waver in our devotion to a noble cause. Your oppressors will not go gently into the night. The

WHEN JESUS CAME TO THE BLACK HILLS
TO DO THE GHOST DANCE
WITH THE SPIRIT OF SITTING BULL

United States has always used terror to subdue those who dare stand against its avaricious desire to gobble up more and more in pursuit of its perverted aims to make all humanity bow before the altar of greed. This nation of evil intentions must face a reckoning. I have done the ghost dance with the spirit of your great leader, Sitting Bull and his strong right arm, Crazy Horse. We shall honour them and all their sacrifices for the great Lakota Nation by completing what they started at Little Big Horn and bring freedom from the oppressors to the sacred Black Hills. Are you ready to die for your right to be free of the tyranny promulgated by the barons of greed who have made you slaves for far too long?"

A deafening roar went up from the crowd. Even the native spies bribed by the government felt a sense of euphoria, and despite their devotion to greed, rather than to the Lakota Nation, they actually wondered if they were on the right side. It was then that they were mystified as Jesus looked into the crowd and pointed at Ben Striker and Daniel Braveman, saying, "Do not harm these two, but escort them out of the compound. And I earnestly tell you Ben Striker and Daniel Braveman, that you can relay to your superiors that a whirlwind is coming."

They wondered how he knew them and how he knew that they were there among the throng.

These were simply two more of the mystified who could not understand the power of this man. For some reason, they looked over at Jesus' disciple, Iudas, who was standing next to them, as if he might have the answer. All Iudus did was look into their eyes with intensity.

Aaron, accompanying the two to assure no harm came to them, said, "Warn your superior this man is not to be taken lightly, and have him tell that buffoon in the White House that it would be better for him to swallow his pride if he wants to avoid bloodshed. Of course, he is one who always avoided real service in uniform to his nation, and will have no qualms about sending others to die, but tell him this time the costs will be extremely high, as was the case twice before when this nation tried to deal harshly with this man. He has unimaginable power that will rain down a cavalcade of hurt on those who are unwilling to compromise and offer the Lakota people the freedom they have always been promised."

Ben Striker, seriousness burned like a brand into his eyes, said with a quivering voice that bespoke of genuine fear of the man whom he had just heard speak, "Who the hell is this guy? I mean really, who is he? We know he aint' no real Jesus."

Aaron replied, "He is the one who will rain down vengeance upon those who are self-seeking and do not honour the truth, but honour unrighteousness. Believe me, there will be wrath and fury as the world has never seen."

Watching the two men walk away, Aaron knew that he had no choice but to serve this man called Jesus. He had no belief in God, so he only looked at Jesus as a mortal, but he saw within him something special in a world where the light of hope had died long ago as capitalism's cult of greed had secured the entire world in its evil web.

He had watched his friend fail twice now in attempts to salvage justice in a land that did not know the meaning of the word, and he wondered how many other times he had failed in pursuit of justice. Why did he not do as most of the world had done, simply give up and accept that in the battle for justice - the war had been won by the wealthy. Evil had triumphed over good and the poor and downtrodden had simply accepted their fate. Che Guevara was the world's last hope, and he had been killed under orders from the USA in Bolivia, where the poor had not been willing to join his fight to unleash them from their chains.

How do you help people who have been slaves for so long that they accept their fate and bow in supplication before their oppressors? If a man has been imprisoned all his life, opening the door to freedom, and showing him the bright sunshine of hope can induce fear, because having others control your life for so long makes a man tremble with trepidation at the mere thought of being in control of his own life.

Jesus had opened the door, and these people were not trembling, because he had aroused something deep inside them that rekindled their noble warrior spirit. But how would they react when they saw their brothers, their sisters, their children, their spouses fall before the hail of bullets unleashed by an army of servile, flag-waving, brainwashed soldiers in service to a nation that demanded conformity? Jesus had a powerful charismatic effect on them now, but how would they react when they watched the agony of death overwhelm those screaming on the battlefield as they fell under the rain of terror promulgated by an army that knew no mercy?

As the helicopters buzzed Lu Ann's car, she was on the phone to the President, crying on the floor of the backseat, finally experiencing some of the fear she and her master had unleashed on so many other Americans. Fearful that her service to this evil man would lead to her death, she pleaded with him to do something to help her, but all he said was, "I will unleash fire and fury."

The helicopters, having instilled fear as intended, scooted away and headed back to the compound to prepare for a battle that would be a defining moment for the Lakota Nation and its newfound pride. The war was about to begin as the President ordered the troops from the 82nd Airborne Division to prepare for an invasion of the Black Hills to quell a rebellion by the Lakota Nation. He was told it would take a few days to muster the 20,000 men and get the equipment ready. He impatiently replied to the general in command, "I want it done quickly. I will not accept anything but the complete annihilation of anyone who stands in the way of that goddamn pipeline that my son-in-law has spent over a billion dollars to put through the Black Hills. If it is delayed, he will suffer financial losses, but the American people will suffer the loss of jobs and the black gold that fuels our economy. My empire and the empire of my family is important to the future of this nation. We are the suppliers of the entrepreneurship that makes America great."

Meantime, the President's advisor called Republican Congressional leaders, who had always bowed before his narcissism in venerating abdication to all he wanted. They had the backbones of jellyfish, which was no backbone at all. Since the Republicans, through a series of gerrymandering over the years, had seized complete control of both houses of Congress and the Presidency, and thereby had appointed a Supreme Court that served only the corporations and the wealthy, the advisor saw no need to include the mealy-mouth Democrats. After all, they had no power any way and were always absent of any backbone either, as they consistently caved in eventually. Thus, the oligarchy that the U.S. government had gradually become would tolerate no one standing in the way of greed.

While Daniel Ormond, the President's assistant, was lining up the spineless obsequious servants to the President's buffoonery, something dramatic was occurring in Sioux Falls and Rapid City. A cadre of Barton's men, along with some Sioux warriors were preparing for a raid on the Air National Guard in Sioux Falls to procure planes and on the huge armoury in Rapid City where they were going to commandeer tanks and artillery pieces. So complacent had the military become that they only had a few guards at the entrance to both facilities, and since it was the National Guard, very few soldiers were on base weekdays.

Lu Ann Luce, like all sunshine patriots, was cowering in fear while her chauffeur frantically drove toward the Rapid City Airport, as she looked to her left and saw a convoy of maybe 30 or 40 cars and trucks whizzing rapidly past her. The vehicles were filled with determined looking burly white and brown men and Native Americans actually wearing war paint on their faces. She was desperately dialling the President's private number when the last car in the convoy pulled beside them and out the front passenger and rear passenger windows she saw two rifles aimed at her as the two men taking that dead aim motioned for her to pull over to the side of the road. She told her driver to stop, and sat shivering with growing fright as the two men on the right side of the car piled out quickly and motioned for her to lower her window while the chauffeur sat motionless as two other men came over and signalled for him to get out, which he did.

The low hum of the window as it rolled down penetrated the quiet of the lonely road for a few seconds until other cars whizzed by, the passengers in them seeming to ignore four armed men standing by the side of the road with rifles pointed at Lu Ann and her chauffeur. After all, why should anyone be concerned? This was America, where people paraded around Wal Mart with semi-automatic rifles on their shoulders and revolvers strapped to their hips. This was the land of Jesus, guns, ignorant morons named Bubba and flag-waving patriots who feared immigrants, which is why they had elected a buffoon to run the country because he had promised to protect white privilege. This was a floundering nation of low information voters who were more concerned about their right to be "packing" and to pray to their beloved Jesus Christ than the right to health care, a decent wage, retirement or any of the other things that were important to the "civilized" world. This was America, the land of the free and the home of the brave, or more accurately, the land of the brainwashed and moral cowards.

Philip Big Bear, with James by his side, said to Lu Ann, "My guess is you are talking to the Golfer-in-Chief. Hand me the phone."

Shaking with fright, she did as told and handed Philip the phone. He was direct and spoke with an irreverent tone. "Is this the narcissistic rich boy who prances around like a peacock in full bloom trying to convince everyone how smart he is when he knows in his heart he is nothing but a rich, privileged, low IQ idiot?"

Indignant with fury, the voice on the other end responded. "Who the hell you think you are talking to me this way? I am the President! This is Lu Ann's phone number you are calling from. How did you get her phone?"

Philip, smiling as he looked down at Lu Ann, said, "I am standing here looking at the arrogant bitch. She is now the prisoner of the Lakota Nation, and one day soon I am going to bring her limo to Washington and drive it up your ass."

He tossed the phone on the backseat as he signalled for Lu Ann to slide over. She had no choice but to obey. They left the chauffeur standing confused by the side of the road and drove off with Lu Ann in the limousine. Philip, sitting beside Lu Ann, smiled and said, "I love riding in style. Thanks for the lift."

While this group was savouring the successful raid on the Rapid City Armoury, outside the Sioux Falls Air National Guard Base, Bartholomew Soaring Eagle, a former U.S. Air Force pilot, was leading a band of Barton's men along with some warriors in a surreptitious reconnoitring of the National Guard Air Base as the sun slowly slipped behind the horizon.

To their delight, only one lone solider stood at the entrance gate, armed with a sidearm. As they pulled their vans behind a nearby 7/11, Bartholomew and Barton's aide-de-camp, Hiram Holiday, turned to a member of the Air Guard unit who had been recruited to join them and asked if this was normal, as he had intonated earlier? He replied, "We are weekend warriors and idiots when it comes to security. As I said, there is one guard and the planes have no locks. Crawl in the cockpit and turn on the APU. The engine will ignite and you are ready to roll."

Bartholomew said to him, "And you have access to the weapons storage areas so we can load these babies up with firepower. "

WHEN JESUS CAME TO THE BLACK HILLS
TO DO THE GHOST DANCE
WITH THE SPIRIT OF SITTING BULL

The weekend warrior grinned and said, "I told you we were idiots. Every plane is loaded with a complete array of weapons, ready to fly. Ever since 9/11, we have flown with our weapons locked and loaded. All 102 planes are ready for combat with six AIM-9 Sidewinder heat-seeking air-to-air missiles and 12 AIM-7 Sparrow radar guided air-to-air missiles. There are 24 small air-to-ground missiles and the 20 millimetre cannon is as precise a killing machine as you can get. They are all loaded too, but I have the keys to all the weapons trucks and the fuel haulers. With the two hundred men on our buses on their way, we will probably not have enough men to get all the trucks and aircraft out, but you can do plenty of damage with what we are commandeering."

As he was finishing his evaluation of what equipment and weapons were available, the four buses pulled in with the rest of the men and the clerk in the store looked out the front window and scratched his head, as if wondering if they would all want coffee. What these men wanted was a way to confront the terror of the U.S. government, and they were about to make the first move in the coming war that was now playing out like a chess match.

Bartholomew, the guardsman and Hiram jumped back into the van and made their way toward the gate. The security guard signalled for them to stop and moved toward the driver's side window. As he did, he got a rifle levelled at him as the driver, Hiram, said, "Ask yourself if it is worth dying to defend the indefensible. Reach for that gun on your hip and my friend in the back will blow your fucking brains all over the pavement."

The young man responded by putting his hands up. He was bound with plastic cuffs, placed in the corner of the guard shack and tied to a horizontal beam.

The smoothness of the operation was so drama-free that some of the men felt let down that there was no resistance. The 102 planes were fired up, and streaked off into the sky as others commandeered fuel trucks, loaded armaments onto half-tracks and headed out the gate for Wounded Knee. Radar screens were lighting up as the jets roared rapidly through the hazy sky. Panic was rapidly spreading among the air traffic controllers and calls went out to officials in Washington who were dumbfounded by what was occurring.

The so-called President was in panic mode as he called in his advisers. Ever since he had been a child, he always had people bail him out of trouble. His father had used his money and power to keep this gigantic failure in everything he did afloat. When his father died, he turned to highly paid crooked lawyers and accountants to save an empire. He was more con man than businessman. His public relations agent played the foolish, celebrity worshiping public like a fine-tuned Stradivarius, convincing them that this was a smart man, when, in reality, he was just a character in a grand staged manipulatory play that hoodwinked the public into believing this idiot would bring America back its glory. That glory had been lost long ago, because people like this man represented the very oligarchy that had destroyed any semblance of economic fairness. Now, he was faced with big trouble as he had sought the aggrandizement of being called President, without realizing that the job actually required more than propping your feet up on a desk and looking important. In reality, he was still that frightened little child who never could please his father. He was scared, but as always, hid it with his bombastic, arrogant demeanour. However, those present knew the real man, knew the lack of any moral core, knew the lack of any innate intelligence and knew that in the end he would act like a child rather than an adult in appraising the situation.

General Jerry McCarty, his National Security Advisor, was not the typical military man who relied on bombs and bullets to solve all problems, as he understood the limits of a military that relied on brainwashed poor patriots to do the fighting in support of the corporate defence industry agenda so the rich and privileged did not have to serve. He preferred negotiation to confrontation, and he had taken on the job as National Security Advisor after three others had resigned or been fired after only 6 months trying to keep the Presidential moron from pushing the nuclear button every time someone angered him. It was a thankless job that caused many sleepless nights just wondering if the idiot was up contemplating nuclear annihilation for one of the countries he had so brazenly described as hellholes filled with poor people who would be better off dead.

He paced up and down in front of the President's desk as he said, "Rashness will not quell this nascent manifestation of a rebellious spirit by the Native Americans."

"What the hell you talking about?" loudly replied the President. "Use some English I can understand."

Shaking his head, wondering how this fool ever managed to get through college, McCarty replied, "In short, do not fuck with people who have nothing to lose."

"What you mean nothing to lose? They will lose their goddamn welfare checks. Contact whoever sends them out and see that they are stopped immediately. The damn redskins have been babied enough. So the white man stole their land. Get the fuck over it already."

A steady stream of advisers were entering the Oval Office now, and as the room filled up, the President eased back in his chair, took a deep breath and said, "I need some sound advice. I say we fucking nuke the whole Black Hills, wipe these damn useless piles of shit off the goddamn map. It'll be a lesson to any of the other tribes that dare to stand against this administration that is dedicated to making this country great again like it used to be."

The head of the Joints Chief, General Fuller, said, "Mr. President, we are not dealing with any ordinary group of rebellious people. We have been aware of a man named Colonel Barton, who resigned his commission about five years ago, and as many as 2000 former veterans of the Iraq and Afghanistan wars making their way to the Lakota Reservation in Canada over the past five years, apparently meeting with some self-styled saviour actually calling himself Jesus. We had spies there, but about a month ago, they simply stopped providing any information. The last communiqué we had simply said, 'We are coming for you.' It is assumed by intelligence that they were either killed or joined with those who had made their way to Canada. We now suspect that the 2000 men, and maybe even more, have made their way to the Sioux Reservation in South Dakota. The last few weeks there have seen strange occurrences around Pine Ridge, weird lights in the sky, rumours of the ghosts of Sitting Bull and Crazy Horse appearing and the return of the ghost dance. These strange events have been multiplying expotentially the past few weeks."

The President pounded the desk and shouted, "Why wasn't I told?"

McCarty, trying desperately to project a calm demeanour, replied, "We tried to tell you Mr. President, but you emphatically said unless it was going to disturb the pipeline, you were not interested. For that reason, we just continued to try and locate our various spies to find out what was going on. Most of our spies have been discovered and are no longer able to get effective information out to us. Others have apparently joined the rebellion.

Shouting, the President was furious. "Goddamn, am I the only competent one around here? Am I the only one who has a fucking brain? I am a graduate of one of the finest schools in the USA. I am as smart as Einstein was when it comes to business, and this is business. I built a fucking empire with only a few hundred million from my father. I am the smartest goddamn man to ever sit in this office, and all I have serving me is fucking morons. I need to do something about this before it gets totally out of hand."

Just as he said, "Before this gets totally out of hand," the special assistant to the President, young, ramrod straight modern-day Nazi, Ernie Stallman, hurriedly barged in shouting, "It has already got out of hand. These fuckers just raided the Air National Guard Armoury in Sioux Falls and made off with 102 F-16's and a shit load of weapons."

Leaning his obese, disgustingly large and saggy frame over his desk and furiously pounding it with intensive ferocity, the President shouted, "Fuck, fuck, fuck."

McCarty very calmly turned to Stallman and said, "What about the other National Guard facilities in North or South Dakota, have they been hit?"

Stunned, Eric Stallman stood speechless shrugging his shoulders, as McCarty said, "Find out, now!"

About a minute later, he ran frantically back into the Oval Office with bad news. "They hit the National Guard Armoury in Rapid City. There are 28 tanks, 30 weapons haulers loaded with armaments for the tanks, 12 tankers with diesel fuel and Lars Rocket launchers being pulled by half-tracks all rolling down highway 44 toward Wounded Knee.

Indicative of how unimportant these cretins considered the soldiers who were at the armoury, not a single one of them asked if anyone was killed in the raid. This was what the leaders really thought of the Americans serving their nation. They were nothing but cannon fodder for the corporate war machine, and the President, rather than worrying about anyone being killed shouted out, "What kind of damn soldiers were these idiots, allowing someone to walk off with all that equipment. It is a disgrace. Make sure everyone knows my predecessor in office caused all this by not paying enough attention to the military. I will not be blamed. You hear me, I will not be blamed."

A stern looking McCarty, no doubt assessing the utter stupidity of the man with whom he was now dealing said, "We need to stop this column from getting to Wounded Knee. It will be at least four or five days before we can effectively muster the 82nd Airborne to full strength and crush these rebellious heathens."

The President's private phone was ringing. He looked at the caller ID and saw it was Lu Ann

Luce. McCarty could see that the idiot didn't have any idea what to do, so he said, "Answer it Mr. President. It may be important."

Almost shaking now, the President uttered, "It's Lu Ann's number. They were rude to me when they kidnapped her."

All there, despite the fact they had dealt previously with this man's utter lack of innate intelligence and his inability whatsoever to assess a problem, stood dumbfounded that a situation fraught with so much peril was in the hands of such an utter idiot. It was like someone had put a nine year old child in the Oval Office and made him President for a day, a week, a year, oh my, for four long years.

Still, he was not answering the phone as it continued to ring, the tone dancing about the room to a tune of ineptitude displayed by a man with no clue on how to solve the problem. Finally, McCarty walked over, picked the phone up off the desk, and said, "Hello, how may I help you?"

Bartholomew said, "Howdy there. I can tell this isn't the President, because you sound like a reasonably intelligent person rather than a blithering idiot. To whom am I speaking?"

"This is General McCarty."

WHEN JESUS CAME TO THE BLACK HILLS
TO DO THE GHOST DANCE
WITH THE SPIRIT OF SITTING BULL

Bartholomew said, as he handed the phone to Colonel Barton, "Here is someone who speaks your language." He then continued, telling Barton, "It is a General McCarty."

"Hello General McCarty. You may remember me. I served under you in Fallujah - Colonel Barton here."

"Yes, I remember you damn well. You once disobeyed a direct order to level a Taliban held village."

"Old problem, general. The same problem most of your men had serving under you. You have no sense of honour. It is water under the bridge, but I do not shamelessly kill women and children. Nonetheless, be assured that I have no qualms about standing, along with thousands of Iraq and Afghanistan veterans, with the Lakota people in demanding justice. We took the armoury with no loss of life on your side. We lost one man. So, you drew first blood. We now have, including the Green Berets and the helicopter crews, along with those we captured in Rapid City, a large number of prisoners. We will treat them well, but they will be in the Wounded Knee Church with us, so any assault will also lead to their deaths along with ours. By the way, we also commandeered a shit load of MANPADS (Man Portable Air Defence Systems) so be forewarned that we will have our soldiers all around the reservation ready to take on your Air Force, and we also have our own air force with 102 planes, manned by well-trained pilots ready for some combat."

McCarty's face grew taunt and distraught with anger, as he said, "You cannot win this war."

Barton calmly replied, " This is a war you might win, but be assured you are going to be in a real war, and we will not surrender. We are all prepared to die for this just cause. When you want to talk, call this number anytime. We have a man named Jesus who will talk terms with you, but tell that buffoon there calling himself President who proclaims himself the world's greatest negotiator that this is not some reality TV show where he always comes out on top. He can't negotiate his way out of this as easily as he did on that damn inane television show he was on."

Barton also had a grim prognostication for McCarty. "Remember that if this convoy is attacked, we have 102 planes that will fill the air to level government installations here in South Dakota. Be very careful."

He hung up the phone, smiled and said to Bartholomew, "Tell the men to prepare the mobile missile launchers. They may be coming after us before we get to Wounded Knee."

WHEN JESUS CAME TO THE BLACK HILLS
TO DO THE GHOST DANCE
WITH THE SPIRIT OF SITTING BULL

McCarty looked worried, and the President was fuming, expecting as he always had, to have others take the blame for any failures. He screamed, "Goddamn it. I need some competent individuals to take control of this situation. I'll fucking push the nuclear button and destroy the Black Hills in the blink if an eye."

His lawyer moved swiftly by his side and whispered in his right ear, "Remember that you have a big interest in a pipeline there, and you and your investors will take a financial bath of huge proportions if you destroy it and any potential for its completion."

The President, whose sole purpose in life was the accumulation of vast wealth, which he equated with success and a way to achieve the aggrandizement he craved, gave those words from his White House Council great credence as he stared in contemplation.

After a long period of silence, he turned to General McCarty. "Damn it, do something. Send someone out to destroy these people. We can't have anyone defying my authority. I am the goddamn President. I need some action taken!"

McCarty had slowly grown weary of serving a buffoon who was a coward when his country was at war in Southeast Asia and he could have served, but his father's wealth and influence allowed him to play tennis and golf while the poor and non-influential slogged through the rice paddies of Vietnam in an illegal and immoral war. Men like the President were the result of a nation that demanded great patriotism from the masses, while allowing the privileged to take a pass. This was the America that had morphed from World War II equanimity into a modern day oligarchy, where those at the top reaped all the benefits while those at the bottom served in ill-fated adventures that filled the coffers of the rich with blood money from unnecessary wars.

McCarty was nearly at the end of his rope, but to walk away now would mean turning momentous decisions over to a man with no heart, no soul, no compassion, no understanding of the power he could unleash that might bring on Armageddon. He had to somehow reach deep within and find the courage to try and take hold of a situation that was rapidly getting out of hand. There were other advisers who did not care for restraint, as the ideology of the supremacy of the white privileged class gave no credence to any complaints by Native Americans. Most of the advisors would have gladly herded the Jews into cattle cars had they been alive during Nazi-led Germany. McCarty ascribed to white supremacy also, but he believed in a more subtle approach to achieving the aim of making sure America stayed white.

WHEN JESUS CAME TO THE BLACK HILLS
TO DO THE GHOST DANCE
WITH THE SPIRIT OF SITTING BULL

That was why he was in the President's cabinet, to assure the ideals of White Supremacy were promulgated, but his approach was much more sublime and less abrasive. He had some decorum that he practiced to give the illusion that he believed in inclusiveness, but in his heart, he lamented the passing of a time when the white man was ruler of all he surveyed in America. He very quickly told the President that attacking the column was not smart as the Sioux had surface to air portable missiles and rocket launchers. He encouraged him to prepare to send in the 82nd Airborne in a few days as a show of strength. Time was on their side.

Again, pounding his desk, the child-like, petulant President, displayed the boorish temperament for which he had become infamous. All that was missing now was a playpen and a diaper.

All in the compound greeted the triumphantly returning raiders sombrely as they gently removed the body of the one casualty. His mother cried uncontrollably, and Jesus consoled her as best he could. The mother embraced Jesus and shouted for all there to hear, "My son died for the Lakota Nation and this man has done the ghost dance with the spirits of Sitting Bull and Crazy Horse. I will also do the ghost dance in support of all we are trying to accomplish here."

WHEN JESUS CAME TO THE BLACK HILLS
TO DO THE GHOST DANCE
WITH THE SPIRIT OF SITTING BULL

All the Lakota there begin to join her in that which Wovoka had done so many years ago trying to arouse a nation to get off its knees. They swayed in unison and the white, black and brown soldiers serving with Colonel Barton joined them in solidarity to the cause. The spirit and dedication swept among them like a tsunami roaring ashore, lifting their spirits in determination to carry on the struggle for which the first of their brethren had given his life.

Aaron and Mary embraced as she said, "Do we have a chance to win this war?"

Aaron replied, "Winning against the privileged class has been a dream since men and women squatted in caves. During those days it was the physically powerful who controlled things. They used that physical strength to make others cower in fear. As time passed, it has now become the wealthy who rule with their economic strength to make the rest of us bow in supplication."

Mary pensively interjected, "But we can win?"

"There were brief moments in history when it looked as if the common person would defeat the moneyed class, a time when hope for economic fairness would finally stand triumphant in testament to the sanctity of social justice, but always the leaders either fell prey to those who assassinated hope or the leaders of the movements were corrupted by power and turned their backs on the people they pledged to serve. The Russian Revolution came the closest to truly giving people social and economic justice, but within a few years of that revolution, its charismatic leader, Lenin, was dead and Stalin, obsessed with power, crushed hope under cruel totalitarianism, even assassinating the architect of the revolution, Leon Trotsky, to assure that once again the people were slaves to the few at the top of the economic order. So, will this time be any different? I have watched this extraordinary man fail twice, so I say the odds are certainly against it succeeding this time, because he is standing against a mighty economic and military terrorist nation that never shows mercy to those who dare stand in its way. The United States is an unforgiving juggernaut of corporate thievery with a military used to spread its insidious evil of greed all over the world. We will, in all likelihood, lose, but losing sometimes ignites a spark of victory when you teach people to get off their knees."

Mary looked deep into Aaron's eyes. "I have already won. I have realized a purpose in my life through this man calling himself Jesus, and above all, I have met you, Aaron Adams."

Aaron took her into his arms and held her close, feeling the warmth of a woman who had rekindled

WHEN JESUS CAME TO THE BLACK HILLS
TO DO THE GHOST DANCE
WITH THE SPIRIT OF SITTING BULL

a fire in him that he long ago thought had died in
the flickering embers of age.

CHAPTER 9
ON YOUR FEET, NOT ON YOUR KNEES

As Jesus lay awake at Wounded Knee,
There came a revelation like a rising sea,
And with great power he sensed what could be,
But he knew there awaited a killing spree.

He saw mass murder marching on its way,
As the evil of a nation could not be kept at bay.
In his mind, he observed things as grim,
And sincere concern overwhelmed him.

The U.S military wielded might,
And devastation was usually the foe's plight,
As on human hearts it did gleefully chew,
Until resistance was practiced by but a few.

WHEN JESUS CAME TO THE BLACK HILLS
TO DO THE GHOST DANCE
WITH THE SPIRIT OF SITTING BULL

It marched to perpetrate a fraud,
And used fear to be awed.
Jesus shed tears, for he wept well,
As mournful sighs fell and fell.

He thought of the little children, who
Round his feet often played to and fro,
And how each one was such a gem,
But the US Military would mercilessly kill them.

And many more destructions played
In this ghastly mental masquerade,
All disguised, even to his eyes,
For he knew among his band were spies.

But he was Anarchy; and he boldly rode
On a white horse, as righteousness flowed.
He was pale now even down to his lips,
As he prepared for the coming Apocalypse.

The following morning there was a scurrying about the compound as the tanks now surrounded the entire area, aiming their deadly guns to repel any attempt to storm the compound. MANPADS rockets in the hands of determined warriors were elevated toward the sky in anticipation of any attack from the air. Mobile missile launchers had been dispersed into the nearby hills, and all there in the compound were just waiting now, waiting for the next move by an idiot who had been foolishly elected to the world's most powerful office by an ill-informed populace who were easily manipulated by the words of a demagogue. Like the Hollywood actor, Ronald Reagan, who began the decline of the middle class when as President he sanctified greed as an enviable trait, this President was also an actor. He was a TV star who had turned his con-artistry into an empire built on quicksand that pulled many people under while he always held onto a lifeline, laughing as the suckers were pulled under. To him, as had been professed by P.T. Barnum, there was a sucker born every minute, and in the last election, he had suckered enough people to be elected.

Only in America is the intellectual, the cerebral thinker dismissed as unrepresentative of the people. The voters wanted one of "them" as their leader, not a man with great depth of knowledge. Well, they were probably right, because as a famous publisher once said, "Never underestimate the stupidity of the American voter," and this time they had certainly gone to the bottom of the barrel to pick the absolutely rottenest apple they could find.

The bombastic narcissist was now pacing about early in the morning as he had four televisions on blaring news of what had happened the night before in Rapid City and Sioux Falls. In his heart, he knew he was a failure in life just as his father had said so many times when he had to bail him out of failed businesses. He had hidden the truth about his wealth from the voters, fabricating his net worth in order to impress himself and others with what he had, because in his warped egotistical mind, a man's worth was judged by the size of his bank account. The truth was that he had lived his entire life on the edge of financial insolvency and the voters were simply not smart enough to digest his failures as a disqualification for the office he held.

Fury was rapidly building within him, while he saw what was happening as another example of his inadequacy to rise to the occasion in a crisis. He needed his advisers to rescue him as they always had.

As the child President paced about, General McCarty realized there was no way out of this situation that would not involve bloodshed. The President was a man of such low intelligence that explaining to him the depth of the problem they faced would simply be an exercise in futility. McCarty was an intelligent man, but he was a man with a character flaw that seemed to flow through the veins of most military men. He firmly believed in American moral superiority, when long ago all that moral depth of character had been sacrificed in pursuit of a foreign policy that tried to impose American values on a world that saw that nation as a pariah of hypocrisy.

WHEN JESUS CAME TO THE BLACK HILLS
TO DO THE GHOST DANCE
WITH THE SPIRIT OF SITTING BULL

Walking up to the pacing President, McCarty said, "The 82nd will bring this to an end. It will be in the field in two days. Meantime, let's negotiate with them to stall for time."

"They are terrorists," shouted the President.

"We know that sir, but we need time right now, time to effectuate an effective strategy to quell this rebellion against the authority of this nation. We need some stalling tactics to convince the public we are trying to do the right thing."

"Fuck the public. They think the way I tell them to think. My followers worship me. I can drop an A-bomb on them Injuns and they'll still love me."

"Sir, you are speaking of maybe 30% of the public that assume that you can do no wrong."

Stricken with intense anger, the president replied, "30%, bullshit! Just fucking fake polls. The same polls said I'd lose the election, and look where I am now. The people love me and my telling 'um like it is. Look at the inauguration I had the biggest crowd in history despite what the news media said. Look at how the Christians love me, because they know I stand with them and the Bible. Every Bubba down in the Bible Belt knows I will bring back God into the public square, so they can pray their way to heaven."

WHEN JESUS CAME TO THE BLACK HILLS
TO DO THE GHOST DANCE
WITH THE SPIRIT OF SITTING BULL

"But, Mr. President," uttered McCarty.

Interrupting him before he could finish, the child in the Oval office, said, "I am the President I tell you – a president beloved by his people, and only scorned by those who cannot face the reality that a successful, smart, prosperous man is now running things. I am giving the wealthy a voice, and the people believe that by respecting the wealthy they are going to get some of their money when it trickles down to those who are meant to serve the more affluent in society, people like me who drive the engines of commerce. Look at all the poor, the uneducated and the teeming masses that put their trust in me. I am their hero. They all want to be like me, because I am a winner."

McCarty suffered through these soliloquies of narcissistic self-aggrandizement day in and day out from a man so mentally challenged that his own family would have had him on the psychiatric coach if it were not for fear of losing their inheritances. This was a dangerous man, and that is why McCarty stayed. Although he was every bit as much a fascist as the President, he still had a minuscule commitment to using common sense in assuring the 1% maintained their control over the masses.

Alas, as this cretin of craftiness huddled with the President preparing for the 82nd Airborne to do their dirty work in the Black Hills, Jesus was among his people, walking with the mother of the slain soldier in a sombre funeral processional. The body was borne toward a traditional scaffold, not the corporate-run funeral home where the family of the deceased is fleeced of their savings by glib-tongued salespeople whose job is to make the family feel they "owe" the deceased a grand send-off. Rather, this day the Lakota were returning to a traditional burial that placed the deceased on a high scaffold and covered him with a warm robe for his journey into the spirit world.

> *Jesus wore no kingly crown,*
> *For in his words greatness was found.*
> *Oh, but he had the mark of mayhem*
> *That sparkled all about him.*
> *With a pace stately and fast,*
> *Over heartbroken land he passed.*
> *Trampling despair in his wake,*
> *He shouted "I will die for your sake."*

Mary whispered to Aaron, "There will be more deaths. Am I right?"

"Oh my, I am afraid that yes there will be many. This land has bled before as this mighty tribe while begging for peace fell before the sabres of the white man. This place has known so much agony perpetrated by a nation that sees people of colour as an impediment to progress. Yes, there will be more dead, but my dear Mary, justice is never given without bloodshed. If you want justice, you have to be willing to die for it, because those in power do not give anyone justice without a fight. Those who expect justice will be given by dropping to your knees and begging for it live in a dream world. Justice is won with a sword, not words."

Doing the dance of death for the dead one, all there waited for Jesus' words. They were about to flow like a raging river roaring through a gorge.

"This young man paid the price so many have paid in the pursuit of justice. He lies here as a testament to what it takes to get justice in this cesspool of greed that rules without compassion."

A mighty roar went up from those present, signalling their intention to fight for justice, as Jesus waved his hand from left to right and continued. "We do not ask for war, but if it comes we are ready to undertake it in the pursuit of justice. This is a nation that can spend billions to put a man on the moon, but it cannot find the money to put a child to bed at night with a full stomach. It can find the money to send soldiers to foreign lands to impose the culture of greed, but when those soldiers return home it cannot find the money to keep them sheltered, clothed or educated. This is a nation that can find money to supply politicians with lavish salaries and parsimonious benefits, but it cannot find the money to provide healthcare to all its people. I say to you that this abomination that rewards those at the top while ignoring those at the bottom must be pounded into a pile of rubble by the righteous forces of justice that are about to rain down upon those in power like a mighty thunder storm rumbling from the heavens of indignation."

And a mighty troop of men came around,
With their trampling shaking the ground,
Waving each soon to be a bloody sword,
In service to anarchy's lord.

And with glorious triumph, they
Let Jesus' words hypocrisy slay,
Drunk as with intoxication
Anarchy had great determination.

O'er all of the revered Wounded Knee,
Rose up those who wanted to be free,
Trampling complacency down.
Suddenly hope had they found.

Those in power would be panic-stricken.
Their hearts would with terror sicken,
Hearing the tempestuous natives cry
For Anarchy they would willingly die.

And with reverence all there came,

J. Wayne Frye 215

WHEN JESUS CAME TO THE BLACK HILLS
TO DO THE GHOST DANCE
WITH THE SPIRIT OF SITTING BULL

Clothed in arms like blood and flame,
And of devotion did they sing,
Making this man's anarchy their king.

Cried they, "We have waited, weak and alone,
For thy coming, oh Mighty One!
Our purses are empty, our swords are cold,
But you can give us glory and makes us bold!"

Twenty thousand well-trained U.S. soldiers
plunged from the sky aboard helicopters and
marched toward Wounded Knee, where Jesus had
now assembled about five thousand determined
followers. The Lakota promptly stood on the
defensive, to combat the superior force moving
their way. They felled a number of trees and set
them in position on the plain, planting IED's
within them. Their army had no generals, but
Colonel Barton was a man who had been passed
over for general many times when he was in the
U.S. Army, because he was judged to not be the
kind of man who would blindly follow orders and
put aside his moral code of honour.

Although Barton was in command of the forces,
it was Jesus everyone looked to for guidance. He
was the moral force that supplied the glue to bind
all there in a cohesive dedication to a noble cause.
He paced about the people calm, resolute and
unafraid. Aaron was by his side and said, "And
what now Chief of Anarchy?"

WHEN JESUS CAME TO THE BLACK HILLS
TO DO THE GHOST DANCE
WITH THE SPIRIT OF SITTING BULL

Smiling, Jesus replied, "We wait. War is often more waiting than fighting. Let us hope that we can wait long enough for that idiot in the White House to perhaps be talked into settling this affair without violence; although, I seriously doubt it. He is a man who places no value on anyone's life but his own. I sincerely think we could capture his wife and children, threaten to behead them and he is such a greedy, uncaring, heartless bastard he would try to sell us the blade to use in the deed. He is a man bereft of a soul. He is as dark a person as ever walked this earth."

Both sides sat on the defensive, neither wanting to advance on the other, each having excellent reason not to attack first. The Lakota Army that possessed deadly weapons now had them aimed at the array of forces that surrounded the compound. Neither army was particularly eager to fight at this time, since the open plain put them both in peril. It was then that Jesus sent an emissary to ask if the commander, General Dumbarton, wanted to have a parley with him to see if an accommodation could be reached.

The emissary faced a man who was cold and stern and had been told by the buffoon in the Oval Office, "We put America first. These damn redskins have fought progress all along. It is time for them to get with the programme or get out. Tell them I will negotiate nothing but their total surrender and acceptance of the fact their day has come and gone. We represent progress and the wealth that comes with it."

As the emissary left the meeting with those harsh words ringing in his ears, he noticed the general on his field phone, obviously relaying what happened to the President. Walking back into the compound, he handed Jesus a note that read, "Your only choice is surrender. In a few minutes, we will send an example of the power you face. Look to the skies and you will see power that will crush your rebellion."

Mirrors lost in the dust of generations past reflect the agony of American natives that saw their lives trampled into oblivion by the evil of racism. White Christian superiority flashed a Bible in the faces of Native Americans and demanded they kneel in supplication before an alien God. Thus, fat and ponderous clouds of soullessness have loomed overhead in the years since the Wounded Knee Massacre, which for the killing of innocent old men, women and children led to the awarding of the most medals of honour in any single engagement. A country that awards medals for cutting babies out of pregnant women's wombs and skewering the foetuses on swords while prancing around with pride in their abominations has no depth of moral character. It represents the deepest pit of depravity in a country that actually believes it is morally superior. This was the same mentality that had subsided for awhile among the majority of Americans, but was resurrected by the con-man in the White House who appealed to people's prejudices and used their ignorance to crown himself Chancellor at the head of an emerging new Third Reich.

At Wounded Knee on this day, thanks to Jesus, a dash of hope in an otherwise dark situation had been sprinkled generously among those who had taken up arms to fight the terrorists masquerading as American soldiers. The Lakota there held the reins of new pride as the clouds above ebbed by ever so slowly, greyish with just a tint of red around the edges as the sun tried to peep through. Each person had wrapped their personal desperations in dark cloaks that kept secret the agonies suffered under the jack-booted foot of oppression.

Looking towards a dying fire near the side of the church, Aaron could see Mary lying over near a tree, head propped up on a satchel as she stared at the rolling clouds above. She, at last, even with the fear of a coming war, had recouped her pride in herself and her nation. Her long, lustrous black hair, falling to one side, brought rushing memories to Aaron of the thrill he felt when he had her in his arms. She smiled at him and her twinkling eyes said "I love you."

WHEN JESUS CAME TO THE BLACK HILLS
TO DO THE GHOST DANCE
WITH THE SPIRIT OF SITTING BULL

Then, suddenly, the tranquility of the moment was shattered as a squadron of F-16's streaked across the sky above like a lightning bolt, flying so low that the reverberations from their jet streams rattled the church and caused the dust to swirl about. They were not going to drop bombs or fire a shot. Rather, Colonel Barton shouted, "Do not be alarmed. It is only a show of force!"

This was what General Dumbarton had arranged while the emissary was returning to the compound. As the 12 jets soared above the nearby hills and made sweeping turns back toward the compound to solidify the fear they were trying to instil, out of the skies to the north came what looked like fifty or sixty other F-16's, and the people assumed they were about to be bombarded by an overwhelming force, but Thaddeus, Matthew and Simon shouted in unison, "Look, look, look on the sides of those planes."

The sight sent shivers up and down thousands of spines as the Lakota there stood in awe at the symbols that were now clearly visible as the clouds had dissipated and the bright sunshine was glistening off the grey planes. Eyes filled with tears and thousands of voices cheered in glorious recognition of what the Lakota pilots had spent all night doing. They had painted the symbol of the Lakota Nation on every single plane that was now streaking overhead, defying the U.S. Air Force, letting them know they were ready to engage in a battle over the sacred Black Hills. There was no fear among the people, there was only pride in a nation rising up off its knees and confronting force with force. The surprised U.S. Air Force squadron broke off the engagement and high tailed it out of the area when confronted with a superior force. Although only psychological, without firing a shot, the great Sioux Nation had won its first victory in a war led by the man calling himself the Son of Anarchy.

A society that has no locks can tolerate no thief; without paper or other easy record of man's word, it can tolerate no liar and no troublemaker if there is no jail or prison. This was the original Sioux Nation. They lived in complete harmony with one another and with nature, which provided for all their needs. Then, the white man came along with his obsessive greed and first destroyed the buffalo, which had always provided sustenance to the Sioux who used the meat, and then used the hide from that meat for clothing. They did not pursue wealth, because they believed in sharing so all had what they needed, but the white men fenced off large plots of land and claimed it for themselves. Sharing was not part of he white man's creed. This was the white man's genocide against the original inhabitants of America. From 60 million, they shrunk to a mere 800,000 by 1900. It was not Hitler who committed the worst genocide, but rather, the American government that even went so far as to hand out small pox infested blankets in winter on reservations to inflict millions with the disease. Never had an apology for this appalling behaviour been issued, because the USA was a nation that had refined hypocrisy to a fine art. It could always point the finger of condemnation at others, but never at itself. Like the current President, this was a nation that actually believed in its infallibility.

Back at the White House, news of what had happened created a stir in the Oval Office, and the entire cabinet had been called in, and like the lap dogs they were, the first few minutes were spent praising the buffoon who was their commander and chief, as he craved aggrandizement.

The war had begun, although no shots were fired. The haughty President, after getting his praise, said, "I will not be made a laughing stock. We have superior numbers, superior weapons and superior leaders. We will crush this rebellion with no mercy."

With great vulgarity did all there deplore the actions of the rebels. The Joint Chiefs of Staff insisted they could have hundreds of thousands of troops in the field within days. There was one among them though who wanted to exercise caution. The head of the Department of the

WHEN JESUS CAME TO THE BLACK HILLS
TO DO THE GHOST DANCE
WITH THE SPIRIT OF SITTING BULL

Interior, although no friend of the Native Americans, said, "Be very careful. Too much violence could cause a backlash and rally more people to their cause. There are 562 tribes in the USA with over five million Native Americans. You do not want to rile that many people up."

The President shouted, "How many of the goddamn Indians voted for me. They are not part of my base. They voted for Democrats to hand them their goddamn welfare checks. Fuck 'um, blow the bastards all to hell."

The thirty-one year old assistant to the President, Daniel Ormond, a Heinrich Himmler like enabler, interjected, "Hell, yes!"

The President, looked at Ormond, then the Joint Chiefs and said, "He is right. Hell yes! I want these assholes destroyed."

General McCarty interrupted. "Remember they have hostages in that compound."

Ormond shouted, "Collateral damage – fortunes of war."

McCarty replied, "Tell that to their families."

"Nonsense," said the draft-dodging President, "they knew the risk when they joined up."

WHEN JESUS CAME TO THE BLACK HILLS
TO DO THE GHOST DANCE
WITH THE SPIRIT OF SITTING BULL

Over in the far corner was a woman, the only woman in the cabinet, who had sat quietly through the conversation. The U.N. Ambassador, Shirley Post, very meekly said, "Excuse me. May I offer an opinion?"

The President, replied, "Go ahead."

"I do not think anyone here has given serious consideration to how the rest of the world is going to react if we use violence against these people. This will not bode well for international relations."

The President pounded the desk and shouted, "I put America first. Fuck the United Nations."

"If you put America first, sir, you might want to consider how it is going to look when you send in the army against your own people."

Again pounding the table, he replied, "These Injuns are not real Americans. Before the white man showed up they were just a bunch of heathen savages. Why they just want to go back to living in huts, tepees, whatever you want to call them. These people have all made the reservations into shit-holes after we whites gave them the land as a home. They could make something of the reservations, but all they do is complain about their land being stolen. What the hell were they doing with it anyway? They have always stood in the way of progress. They talk that mumbo-jumbo about the goddamn fucking mother-earth and dance around chanting bullshit. Crush the lot of 'um I tell you."

Shirley Post dejectedly hung her head and shrugged her shoulders. She knew those who wanted no negotiations outnumbered her. The cabinet, all but her, were multimillionaires who had been rewarded with positions of authority after working diligently to get one of their own elected. The nation was in the hands of a pack of business tycoons who saw the treasury as their own personal piggy bank and every government entity a hindrance to their designs to make the nation into a corporation and the people into slaves to the wealthy.

What dreary ghosts of hope had fled
While a nation sunk, as revolutionaries bled.
There was one who stirred hope many saw.
Jesus at Wounded Knee declared war
And rose up with pride to sound the clarion call.
His plans were to make the mighty fall.

Ah, but the President wanted a wall,
For he heeded the bigot's call
As a way to gain grandeur and fame
This man lost in narcissism's frame.
He groaned and smote in his breast
Without any thought for those oppressed.

J. Wayne Frye   225

WHEN JESUS CAME TO THE BLACK HILLS
TO DO THE GHOST DANCE
WITH THE SPIRIT OF SITTING BULL

Evil one, he wanted to hear foes' cries
To echo loudly in the blood red skies.
To see lances pierce their brown skin
Would on his wicked face put a grin.
He craved battle's piercing roar
And the clamouring thunder of war!

"If it wasn't for that pipeline I'd nuke those goddamn red devils," bellowed he President.

Most there were obedient lap dogs who, for their own selfish reasons, catered to the egomania of this despicable man who was about to make one more of his many miscalculations in a life filled with miscalculations. He stood up and said to the Joint Chiefs, "Obliterate those bastards. Spare not one bullet to bring them to their knees."

Like the President, these men had no character. The overpaid, overambitious, overbearing, over-praised warmongers nodded in agreement to use the U.S. military once again as an instrument of ethnic cleansing on American soil.

In the compound, Jesus was huddling with those who were leaders among troops where there were no leaders, just some who knew more about battle than others.

Barton said to those gathered there. "If we strike first, we will be the aggressor and public opinion will probably swing against us. We must prepare for the worst, but striking first is not an option if we want to win the American people's hearts and minds."

It was at that very moment that a frantic woman came running over to those huddled in a circle there outside the church. She excitedly shouted, "The news networks are all here. What should I tell them?"

Jesus looked at Aaron. "Tell them Aaron Adams will talk to them. I do not want to appear as one who seeks the spotlight. I am not here to reach out to all oppressed Americans right now. I am here to fulfill that which I have been called to do, lead the Lakota into the bright sunshine of hope and get them off their knees."

A reluctant Aaron knew that to argue against his being the spokesperson would be an exercise in futility. He rose and said, "Thanks a lot," as he walked away.

Walking outside the compound entrance where the news trucks had been permitted to come within a few hundred feet of the compound, one of the news people there, Candy LaCraw, having covered many of Aaron Adams' escapades shouted, "It's Aaron Adams, New York private eye, who was with that guy Jesus in New Jersey."

WHEN JESUS CAME TO THE BLACK HILLS
TO DO THE GHOST DANCE
WITH THE SPIRIT OF SITTING BULL

As they all frantically shouted questions, Aaron moved before them and said, "I'll make a statement and that will be it. Please let me speak."

Before he could utter a word, the reporter from Fox News, mouthpiece of the administration shouted, "Rumour is that fake messiah calling himself Jesus is behind this ridiculous affront to law and order. Is that true?"

Aaron, not one to mince words, replied, "Listen you mouthpiece for fascism, I'll make a statement and leave it at that. No matter what I say, you will misconstrue it to fit your own narrative, because you are the real fake news, not those others here in front of me who try to be fair and balanced."

As the Fox reporter glared at him with disdain, Aaron began. "First, fake messiah or not is for people other than me to decide. All I know is that a man whom I have known for many years calling himself Jesus is among these people who have grown weary of being oppressed by a nation that stole their birthright, stole their self-respect, stole their land. These people have been joined by sympathetic veterans of American wars of conquest to stand shoulder-to-shoulder with them in solidarity against a pack of corporate capitalists who have no respect for the mother-earth and want to bring even more destruction to this land considered sacred by these people."

WHEN JESUS CAME TO THE BLACK HILLS
TO DO THE GHOST DANCE
WITH THE SPIRIT OF SITTING BULL

"The Lakota, at this time, send a call out to all Native Americans, and to all Americans of every race and creed who value freedom and respect for the law to join them in demanding that the U.S. government, after all these years, fulfill its obligations under the treaties it has signed with the Lakota people. There will be no compromise. These people have had enough of promises and enough of a nation that feels it does not have to honour agreements. America uses the term terrorists often to describe those who perpetrate heinous acts against the vulnerable. Well, look all around Pine Ridge, and you can see the real acts of terrorism by the United States against these people. Terrorism takes many forms. Any nation this wealthy that allows the obscene poverty we see day in and day out, any nation that demands a child be born, but refuses to provide that child with healthcare, food and shelter, any nation that can spend trillions on endless wars but not find money to take care of its elderly is an abomination, any nation that had rather build walls than bridges is a blight on the sanctity of humankind."

"America has practiced genocide of the vilest kind right here at Pine Ridge. It has slaughtered innocent old men, women and children and had the nerve to award medals to those who cut babies out of mother's wombs and paraded them around on sabres. The people of this nation have been propagandized into believing in its moral superiority. The truth is this is a nation of hypocrites who refuse to see the evil they have perpetrated in the name of greed and self-righteousness. We say to the soldiers who are surrounding us now, prepare to die just as we are prepared to die, or, you can walk forward, join us and take a stand against the evil that is seeping out of the halls of a government that long ago stopped representing the people and only represents those who buy influence with their 30 pieces of silver."

"Treason," shouted the Fox News reporter.

Aaron pointed directly at him, and said, "Treason is when a journalist sacrifices his integrity for cash from an organization that is the mouthpiece for oppression. Treason is when you see a nation committing atrocities and stand in silence."

All the other reporters broke out in applause as Aaron turned and walked back toward the compound, where Jesus stood at the entrance, greeted him with a smile and said, "Keep at it and one day you may be as spellbinding as I am."

Hear Jesus omnipotent, all wise, all great
To whom all fate and folly seems known.
Could this man actually be divine,
As it seems all he does is a sign.

J. Wayne Frye   230

WHEN JESUS CAME TO THE BLACK HILLS
TO DO THE GHOST DANCE
WITH THE SPIRIT OF SITTING BULL

Behold among the people the bravery he decree.
Be thine the judgment, for all there bend to thee.

And thus a halo appears, and there are replies,
While pealing thunder shakes the groaning skies.
He walks by and hope in all is driven,
Resounding throughout Lakota heaven.
Aloft in air sublime the echo rode,
And a new pride resides in each abode.

Son of Anarchy hath come to let the coward die,
And his anger against evil is let fly.
Son of Anarchy, all there did obey,
Listening intently to everything he had to say.
Suddenly, all there the ghost dance began,
Invoking the glory of Sitting Bull again.

There are raging elements within the hearts of
men, which, on occasion, can make the spirit soar
with euphoric splendour. At that very moment,
Barton's men joined in doing the ghost dance with
the Lakota, because all were one now, all sensed
that they were about to go into battle against a
superior enemy who knew not the meaning of
mercy. Yet, they were united in a cause that had
once stirred the mercurially cerebral and grand
strategist Sitting Bull to encourage his most
accomplished warrior, Crazy Horse, who believed
no white man's bullet could kill him in battle, to
destroy Custer's 7th Army at Little Big Horn in
what was the greatest Native American victory.

J. Wayne Frye   231

WHEN JESUS CAME TO THE BLACK HILLS
TO DO THE GHOST DANCE
WITH THE SPIRIT OF SITTING BULL

Aaron gently, with great affection, held Mary's hand and they danced together, feeling a part of something grand and glorious, something that swelled them with pride. It was then that Jesus stood on the church steps, under the cross that towered over the entrance, and bade all there give him their attention.

"I say to you that the angel of death is with us. It has come to flap its wings over our enemies as we are about to enter a great battle. While raging waves of hate beat in the hearts of those in the White House, know that not all those we are about to face harbour hatred for the Lakota. We can hope that many men among the army facing us, the enlisted men, the men who always do the fighting and dying, while the privileged pull the levers of power, may well see that they are engaged in an illegitimate and immoral war against a sovereign people. Like so many brave men during the Vietnam era, they may throw down their weapons and flee to Canada before sacrificing themselves for the lunacy of a nation dead set on imposing the culture of greed on the entire world."

"This compound reverberates with the sounds of tumultuous thoughts, as within our bosoms raises the call to the glory of a noble cause. The polished wheels of indignation turn on the axels of determined souls who will not yield. We shall move the gates of hell that lie before us and fight the devils of Washington who embrace the evil of greed and aggrandize it as an enviable trait. The evil on the Potomac towering in might shall fall, and we shall bury hypocrisy beneath that abominable one small wall that will remain from that big wall that the creature of privilege in the Oval House has demanded as a monument to his bigotry. That wall will be his tombstone of infamy, as we bury the evil he has perpetrated and isolate it in a prison of loathing with all those who have bowed before his racism and embraced it with intense vigour."

Jesus paced about now and he gazed upward, pointing into the sky as he said, "There, above us is not heaven, for what crazy man believes in some fairy-tale land in the sky where angels with wings pluck harps and sit upon fluffy clouds in celestial blissfulness? This heaven paved with streets of gold was invented by the privileged class to keep people in bondage, keep them believing in some fairy tale land where they will get all they were denied here on earth. The church has for centuries been an accomplice to capitalistic evil with a narrative that allows the enslavement of the masses, justifying poverty as if it somehow makes you holier. There is nothing holy about a child going to bed hungry at night. There is nothing holy about the rich riding by in their chauffeured limousines as people lie on the streets without shelter. There is nothing holy as hospitals turn away the sick because they cannot afford to pay. There is nothing holy in promoting greed as an enviable trait. There is nothing holy in a man who sits in the White House and robs widows, orphans and the working class so he can hand tax breaks to himself and his rich friends. There is nothing holy about a nation that hypocritically tells other nations they may not have weapons of mass destruction while it sits upon the largest cache of weapons of mass destruction in the world. Who appointed this nation the moral guardian of the earth, a nation that has committed the single greatest genocide in history?"

"There was one grand shining moment when the Lakota, with their allies the Northern Cheyenne and Arapaho swept down like avenging angels and annihilated George Armstrong Custer and the men who aided with dedicated glee his evil intentions to destroy the Indian Nations with cold, calculated precision. Today, we are facing an army led by General Dumbarton, who is every bit as cold and calculating as Custer, and he answers to a man in the White House who has sat on a throne of evil since he popped out of his mother's womb. He grew up as a child of privilege and has used that privilege to cut a devastating swath through life, showing absolutely no concern for the damage he does in piling up riches on the backs of people he tramples beneath his greed. The world is a dangerous place to live as long as men like him are foolishly put in control by those too ignorant to see evil when it is staring them in the face. Still, I say to you that there is an evil much worse. That is the complacency of those who see evil and do nothing about it. This nation is now on the same path that Nazi Germany took. Good people are standing by as this man tries to silence those who challenge his immense evil. Just as good Germans did absolutely nothing as they watched their Jewish neighbours being hauled off to concentration camps; good Americans are now watching as immigrants, non-Christians and people of colour are being singled out by a man who has put the foxes in charge of the hen houses."

The crowd was hanging on every word now, because Jesus' spellbinding oratory was piercing the complacency that had for so long trapped these noble people in a slumber that allowed the lions of greed and bigotry to devour them without a fight. As Mary looked into Aaron's eyes, he smiled and said, "He is not through. There is a kicker coming that will seer the hearts of these people and plant a seed which will grow into a mighty oak with thick, hard branches that will not bend before the adversity coming this way. I have seen it before, seen the power he has to kindle a fire of indignation in people that even the cold hand of death cannot douse."

WHEN JESUS CAME TO THE BLACK HILLS
TO DO THE GHOST DANCE
WITH THE SPIRIT OF SITTING BULL

Looking again skyward, Jesus continued. "The evil ones on the plains before us and in Washington depend on fear to keep the populace in line. They have used propaganda and brainwashing to make these soldiers believe in the high moral character of a nation that, in reality, has the morality of a coiling rattlesnake in the hot noonday sun ready to strike with the poison of self-righteous arrogance. The lowly soldier is, in his heart, maybe lacking of evil intent, but he has turned his power to think over to merchants of mayhem who only can stay in control by turning people against one another, turning the Christian against the Muslim, turning the white man against the black man, turning the middle class against the poor, turning the uneducated against the educated, turning the native born against the immigrant. Fear is their only means of control and today none of you should fear any man, because you stand at a crossroads of hope that may end in defeat, but you will be defeated on your feet, not on your knees."

CHAPTER 10
TO HEAR THE SONG OF FOOLS

*The President, in his mind, wore a kingly crown;
In his evil, greedy grasp a dark sceptre shone;
On his forehead was the mark of Cain some saw.
Yet, too many saw God and King, above the law!*

*The U.S.A. o'er many countries from sea to sea
Passed its evil while thinking it was free,
Tearing up countries, trampling freedom down
Until it destroyed town after town.*

*Its army that made people panic-stricken,
Loving to make the conquered with terror sicken,
But now they faced those with a tempestuous cry
Who followed the son-of-anarchy willing to die.*

J. Wayne Frye　　　　　237

WHEN JESUS CAME TO THE BLACK HILLS
TO DO THE GHOST DANCE
WITH THE SPIRIT OF SITTING BULL

America's military, with pomp always came,
Clothed in armaments like blood and flame,
Corporation hired murderers who did sing,
That their President was God, Law and King.

But they were facing the Son-of-Anarchy now,
A man who before no one would ever bow.
He aroused the natives with what he had to say,
Promising with Anarchy, they'd have a better day.

The preservation of peace and the guaranteeing of man's basic freedoms and rights require courage and eternal vigilance: courage to speak and act, and if necessary, to suffer and die for truth and justice.

Aaron was a man who had given up any hope of justice in the America he had seen end an immoral war in Vietnam, only to embrace the immoral war against the poor and middle class conducted by corporations and the wealthy who saw people, not as human beings, but as assets to feed the bottom line. He had tried valiantly for so many years to believe in hope, but as he watched the people consistently vote against their own interests by falling for manipulative patriotic babble and religious subterfuge, he simply gave up. Yet, he saw hope in this man calling himself Jesus, as he realized that throughout history it has been the inaction of those who could have acted; the indifference of those who should have known

J. Wayne Frye

better; the silence of the voice of justice when it mattered most that made it possible for evil to triumph. Thus, his scepticism was tempered by the knowledge that he could savour little victories along the perilous path he trod day in and day out in the underbelly of society while engaging in a profession that exposed him to the seedy side of life. He looked at Mary and took her hand, for he had found in her a new vigour for life. He wanted to show her he appreciated her as a woman who was standing up for justice in a world that had beaten her down with indifference. She was just another victim in a society with no compassion.

Aaron smiled at her and said, "We have been neglecting intimacy of late, but I want you to know that no matter what happens you have rekindled in me a zest for life that was gone. You are an extraordinary woman Mary Morning Dove."

She smiled, tilted her head onto his right upper arm and whispered, "I know a spot."

Saying nothing, only smiling, Aaron let her take his hand and pull him toward a rendezvous with passion. Behind the church was a small building where extra ammunition was stored. Mary reached into her pocket and pulled out some keys, holding them up and dangling them in front of her very broad smile. She reached down, put one of the keys in the padlock and turned it as she whispered, "Unlocking the door to my love tunnel that you are about to drive into and discover the warmth of my wantonness."

As soon as they walked in she gently closed the door, and the two of them slid a large box in front of it. She removed all her clothes as quickly as a jackrabbit jumping out of a briar patch while Aaron was doing the same, but much slower as he could not take his eyes off the magnificent form of a woman that stood before him. She was glowing like a diamond sparkling in the noonday sun. Her dark black hair cascaded down over her shoulders as she propped her right leg up on the box in front of the door and pushed her left leg as far to the left as possible so that Aaron could longingly gaze at the wide open love canal that sat so stately within a huge patch of dark pubic hair that looked like a giant forest of pleasure. She cupped her huge breasts in her hands, jiggling them as the nipples became rock hard. Aaron moved to her, reached around and grabbed her shapely ass, pulling her close to him. She did not altar her stance, as being wide open between her legs allowed his rock hard member to slide easily into her moist warmth.

Aaron began to pump furiously as he vigorously pounded Mary's love canal like he was boring a hole into a mine filled with the world's greatest treasure. Mary's burning flesh seemed to spring into its fullest conformations as she was now meeting each thrust with grand enthusiasm. She began shaking as Aaron kept massaging her ass cheeks. Mary's flesh shook and quivered under the emphatic skill of Aaron's smooth rhythm. Her eyes closed and her lips parted, longing for a warm kiss. Their mouths met and tongues duelled like two fencers facing off in the Olympic finals.

Mary played with her erect nipples. Then her hands swam down along her flanks. She rubbed her hips. She rose on her feet and they pointed like ballerina's as her toes curled. Her pelvis rose in unison with Aaron's mighty thrusts as both their bodies rippled like a wave on the sea. The air was filled with frantic moans as cries of ecstasy emanated from both lovers, and spasmodic spurts of joy juice slammed violently into Mary like bullets rapidly popping from the barrel of a gun, only these bullets were pounding deep into the soul of a woman who was exploding into orgasmic ecstasy as each spurt into her warm hole was like a magic wand wielded by a wizard of pleasure.

They collapsed in each other's arms and eased down onto the box, just sitting there silently trying to catch their breath. Mary smiled and said, "That was the fuck of a lifetime."

Aaron smiled back and replied, "Any more fucks like that, and my life will be over."

WHEN JESUS CAME TO THE BLACK HILLS
TO DO THE GHOST DANCE
WITH THE SPIRIT OF SITTING BULL

They laughed, dressed and slid the box of weapons away from the door. As they stepped out, standing there in front of them was Jesus. He was smiling, as he said, "I didn't want to interrupt, so I thought I would wait until you were finished."

Aaron said, "I can see by the look on your face, there is a problem, and whenever you have a problem, somehow it means trouble for me."

"We need to talk," replied Jesus.

Mary sensed that this was a private matter so she said, as she tuned and walked a way, "I'll see you guys later."

Jesus put his left arm around Aaron as they began to stroll toward the nearby creek. He was pensive as he said, "Only in America Aaron could you be pro-death penalty, pro-war, pro unmanned drone bombs, pro-nuclear weapons, pro-guns, pro-torture, pro land-mines, pro-corporate run health care, and still hypocritically, when it comes to abortion, call yourself pro-life. This simply is a nation that frankly is the most backward place in the world, run by people who have refined the art of calling themselves Christians to get votes, and then never doing anything at all that is Christian, while their voters continue to support the most anti-Christian policies imaginable. Christianity in this country is more about hating than loving.

J. Wayne Frye   242

WHEN JESUS CAME TO THE BLACK HILLS
TO DO THE GHOST DANCE
WITH THE SPIRIT OF SITTING BULL

There are a few pockets of sanity, but far too few. I have usually been a good judge of character, but sometimes people fool even the son-of-man. I may have made a mistake, because I placed my trust in a man named Dr. Myron Morrison, a renowned nuclear scientist who claims to be a Christian, and I have usually avoided those kind of people, because I find atheists more compassionate, more sympathetic to the plight of the poor, more anti-war, more dedicated to progress than those who pray to God but are hypocrites without a real commitment to the betterment of humanity."

"Welcome to the real world. It's a bitch!"

"Let me share something with you Aaron. It is something you, as an intelligent man are probably aware of, but be patient and let me lay out the scenario in my own way, so you will understand. The loss of an atom bomb is not as rare an occurrence as one would hope. The American Defence Department has confirmed the loss of 11 atomic bombs. It is believed that up to 50 nuclear weapons worldwide were lost during the Cold War. Most of these highly dangerous weapons are still lying on the ocean floor. In 1989, a fire on board a Russian submarine resulted in its sinking in the North Atlantic Ocean, together with two torpedoes and their nuclear warheads. In 1968, another nuclear submarine, the USS Scorpion, sank to a depth of 3,300 meters (10,800 feet) about 320 nautical miles south of the Azores. There were two nuclear warheads on board. Because of the considerable depths involved, neither the weaponry nor the nuclear reactors on both submarines have been recovered. A much larger number of atom bombs disappeared in plane crashes over the open ocean. Between the late 1950s and mid-1960s, the most explosive part of the Cold War, U.S. bombers carrying atom bombs were in the air around the clock, 365 days a year. Their four main routes passed over Greenland, Spain, the Mediterranean, Japan and Alaska. Only when the bombers became capable of flying across the Atlantic or Pacific on one tank of fuel did the frequency of accidents diminish. Probably the most absurd broken arrow (the Americans' code word for accidents involving nuclear weapons) happened in 1965 on board the USS Ticonderoga. The aircraft carrier was in route from Vietnam to Yokosuka in Japan when a fighter-bomber emerging from one of the giant elevators that carry the aircraft from the ship's hold onto the deck plunged into the ocean. The pilot, the aircraft and the nuclear bomb on board sank to a depth of five kilometers (16,400 feet) and were never found. That incident was also kept secret for many years, partly because, when it was finally made public in 1981, it proved that the Americans had stationed nuclear weapons in Vietnam, with every intention of using them until President Nixon gave up on the war because he was fighting impeachment. The U.S. military's rather nonchalant handling of its most dangerous toys was not limited to foreign waters. In fact, seven of the 11 nuclear warheads that are officially missing were lost in the USA. In 1958, a bomber pilot had to jettison the hydrogen bomb he was carrying after colliding with a fighter jet. The bomb then disappeared in the shallow waters of Wassaw Sound, about 20 kilometres (12 miles) from Savannah, Georgia. A determined scientist searched for years and found that bomb."

A light flicked on in Aaron's head. "Dr. Myron Morrison. However, you are not through. There is always more to the story."

"Bingo," replied Jesus, as he continued. "The crew of a B-52 that exploded in 1961 as a result of a defective fuel line was less fortunate. Before the aircraft broke apart, the men managed to eject their dangerous cargo. One of the two hydrogen bombs was parachuted safely into a tree, while the other one went down in a swamp near the small city of Goldsboro, North Carolina, where it plunged an estimated 50 meters (165 feet) into the marshy ground and disappeared to never be found. At least that is what officials think."

Aaron interjected, "Morrison has both of those bombs. They are operational and you are working with Morrison."

WHEN JESUS CAME TO THE BLACK HILLS
TO DO THE GHOST DANCE
WITH THE SPIRIT OF SITTING BULL

"Bingo again my friend."

Jesus removed a map from the back pocket of his blue jeans. He unfolded it and pointed at an area right on the North Dakota and South Dakota border. "On the farm of a man named Robert Soaring Eagle are two missile silos from the Cold War. They are assumed to be deactivated and empty, but they are not. Within one of those side-by-side silos is Dr. Myron Morrison, who has been surreptitiously assembling two nuclear bombs atop two Honest John SS-25 rockets for nearly four years now. They are ready to fly!"

"Target – Washington, D.C. if things go south here," said Aaron.

Jesus, with an very serious tone, replied, "Well, we know that the moron sitting in the White House with that little black case is capable of unspeakable acts. He must be convinced that there is no victory over the Lakota without paying a price that even an idiot like him may not be willing to pay. We hope."

Aaron could not resist, because, despite being a firm nonbeliever and having distaste for the hypocrisy practiced by believers, he knew his Bible well. He winked at Jesus and said, "From Ecclesiastes: It is better to hear the rebuke of the wise, than for a man to hear the song of fools."

CHAPTER 11
THEY WIND UP BEING CHANGED
BY THE DEVIL

*Between the mighty Lakota and their foes
A mist, a light, an image from behind rose,
Small at first, and weak and frail,
Like the vapour of the vale.*

*Clouds did grow crimson like a furnace blast,
Like tower-crowned giants striding fast,
And glare with lightning did fly,
And speak in thunder to the clouding sky.*

*A vision grew, a shape arrayed without fail
Brighter than the viper's scale,
And up-borne on wings whose grain*

WHEN JESUS CAME TO THE BLACK HILLS
TO DO THE GHOST DANCE
WITH THE SPIRIT OF SITTING BULL

Was as light as that of rain.

With step as soft as wind the vision passed
O'er the heads of men below so very fast
That they knew the presence was there,
And looked and looked into the air.

As earth beneath the visions waken,
As stars from night's loose hair are shaken,
As neck hairs arise when loud winds call,
Thoughts sprung of how their enemies would fall.

And Anarchy the gallant Lakota to defend
Welcomed the Horse of Death, tame-less as wind.
Other ghostly horses on hoofs did grind
As they formed line after line.

A rushing light of clouds and splendour,
A sense awakening, and yet tender
Was heard and felt. At its close
A mighty war cry arose.

Lakota men and women of glory
Were about to be heroes of a grand story,
As they rose like lions after slumber,
In un-vanquishable, un-fearful number.

Now, I am but a scribe relating the story of a
man who came among the Lakota and led them in
their greatest battle since Little Big Horn. I am a
profound disbeliever in all religion. The Christians

think they have a monopoly on virgin births, but the truth is that Lord Krishna and Buddha, as well as many others were supposedly born of a virgin. Of course, we westerners are supposed to believe only Jesus was the one true virgin birth. It is amazing that you can tell an adult that Santa Claus is a fairy tale and they will understand, but try to convince them that Jesus is a fairy tale and they will call-out the minions of hell to lay you low in the darkest pits of that "real hell" that is down in the bowels of the earth. One Pope once uttered, "We have a great thing going in this Jesus Christ myth – keep it up." The church harbours almost as many scoundrels as one can find on Wall Street, and they do as much damage. I mention this with a sincere apology to those who are devoutly religious, but no matter how religious a person might be, I do believe they are capable, if they will only open their hearts and above all their brains, to admitting that scoundrels often hijack religion just as they have hijacked the U.S. government. One need look no further than the Oval Office on this eventful day to see how a man with no moral core was pacing about using God as an excuse for violence to bring the Lakota back on their knees in supplication to his will. He was as irate as a child throwing a tantrum when he declared, "God made me President. He ordained me to lead this nation back to its greatness. I am the only hope for this country and still over half the people stand against me and my grand plans for a resurrection of our glory. These damn Lakota and this moron calling himself Jesus are trying to keep me from fulfilling God's plan for this great nation. Annihilate the bastards. I tell you do it now. Order the army in, the air force, level the town of Wounded Knee and eliminate that blight to progress once and for all. Now I say, now!"

McCarty very deliberately said, "Are you sure?"

"I am the goddamn President. When I give an order I expect it to be obeyed." He looked over at the black box with the nuclear codes as he said, "And order a retargeting of one fucking missile for Wounded Knee, now!"

McCarty nodded almost apologetically at Daniel Ormond who immediately got on the secure line to Command Central and ordered that one missile be re-programmed for targeting Wounded Knee as the President pushed the verification code by putting his thumb on the pad that verified the order was coming from him.

The President was in one of his childlike frenzies pacing up and down. McCarty, every bit the fascist his commander and chief was, but a man who could calculate circumstances from a more adult approach, decided to humour the President while promoting the use of traditional military forces to quell the rebellion.

WHEN JESUS CAME TO THE BLACK HILLS
TO DO THE GHOST DANCE
WITH THE SPIRIT OF SITTING BULL

He moved to the desk and as the President paced, said, "The 7th Air Calvary has swept into the area on their choppers and have 20,000 men ready to charge. They can get the job done without resorting to a nuclear option."

The President, a man totally ignorant of history, had once seen the Earl Flynn movie, *They Died with Their Boots On*, and although he could not even remember the words to the National Anthem, he could remember movies. He blurted out, "Wasn't the 7th Calvary Custer's outfit?"

"It was, yes sir."

"Goddamn, they got their asses kicked!"

"It was a different time Mr. President. General Dumbarton will get the job done."

Puffing out his chest, leaning over and pounding the desk with his famous little hands, he said, "He better get it done. I will not tolerate failure."

McCarty picked up the President's white phone, and told the head of the Joint Chiefs of Staff to give the order to attack. The die had been cast, and it was a dark die that would rain down on the Black Hills with a fury that could only be stayed by divine intervention, because the U.S. Army was about to unleash hell on its own soil.

WHEN JESUS CAME TO THE BLACK HILLS
TO DO THE GHOST DANCE
WITH THE SPIRIT OF SITTING BULL

On the day of this great confrontation between the Lakota and the U.S. Army, as always, among the American troops were chaplains trained in the art of assuring those about to enter battle that God was on their side. Invoke the name of God along with the glory of the waving American flag and shivers run up and down soldiers' spines as they are convinced they are noble representatives of God in a great nation blessed by him. This indoctrination begins the first day of school for every child in America, where, just like the Nazis in Germany, the youth are brainwashed and programmed to serve the ruling elite and corporations by dutifully standing and reciting the lines, "I pledge allegiance to the flag of the United States of America and to the Republic for which it stands, one Nation under God, indivisible, with liberty and justice for all." Thus, a steady stream of cannon fodder represented by impressionable youth is instilled with the belief in the superiority of a nation that has the highest poverty rate in the First World, is the only First World nation without universal healthcare, is the First World nation with the lowest tax rate for the wealthy, is the First World nation with the longest work week, is the First World nation with the most weapons owners because it is easier to get a gun than a driver's licence, and finally is the nation that committed the greatest terrorist acts of all time with the brutal, heartless atomic bombing of Hiroshima and Nagasaki.

WHEN JESUS CAME TO THE BLACK HILLS
TO DO THE GHOST DANCE
WITH THE SPIRIT OF SITTING BULL

This book is not an ideological endeavour, so I will not spend too much time on trying to question the ideology of a nation that is filled with those who thump a Bible in one hand while holding a gun in the other. However, in order to understand what happened, we must explore the idea of the intervention of the super-physical order in the affairs of the physical order. My readers will be mistaken if they suppose that I think miracles in the Bible are credible but miracles in the Black Hills are incredible. I hold no such absurdities. But I confess, very frankly, that I did not see what happened, but am only relating a third-hand account of one of history's most incredible events. So I absolutely say, not that super-normal interventions are impossible, nor that they have not happened, but I have simply never seen one first-hand.

Tis to hunger for war's diet,
As the rich President in his riot
Casts to the poor soldiers that lie
Ready to suffer beneath his cruel eye.

Tis to let the ghost of Black Hills' gold
Take from toil of the Lakota a thousand fold,
More than ever any substance could
Tyrannies of those who do not know good.

Paper money that is forgery
Of the title deeds to land hold ye.

J. Wayne Frye   253

WHEN JESUS CAME TO THE BLACK HILLS
TO DO THE GHOST DANCE
WITH THE SPIRIT OF SITTING BULL

Why not hold something of worth?
The Lakota's inheritance is Mother Earth.

And at length when the poor complain,
With a murmur weak and vain,
'Tis to see the tyrant's crew
Ride over your wives, children and you.

Then it is to feel revenge,
Fiercely thirsting to exchange
Blood for blood and wrong for wrong
As Jesus makes the Lakota strong!

The sun peered out from behind clouds as Air Force jets streaked overhead, and dipped down for a simulated bombing run. Thus began what was on the most awful day of that awful time, on the day when ruin and disaster came so near that their long shadows cast ominously over the sacred Black Hills. However, the intense darkness and more importantly, the grand glory of this day would reverberate all around the world. There was an agony seeping into the souls of the Lakota army, for they knew that this battle would probably end in defeat, but they would not be deterred from going forward to meet their fate.

On this dreadful day, then, when the U.S. Army was preparing to have 20,000 soldiers storm the Lakota compound after rolling in heavy artillery that swelled like a storm of evil which would probably devastate the compound filled with Lakota faithful, it was evident that not only would the Lakota be defeated, but utterly annihilated. Suddenly, the American guns thundered and shrieked against the Lakota who held the village of Wounded Knee. The Lakota joked at the shells, and found funny names for them, and had bets about them, and greeted them with chants. The shells came on and burst, and tore good Lakota from limb to limb, and as the heat of the day increased so did the fury of that ceaseless artillery attack. There was no help it seemed until Colonel Barton, who wanted to lull the opposing army into the belief that there would be no return fire, signalled for the tanks and the artillery around the compound to begin firing.

There comes a moment in a storm at sea when people say to one another, "It is at its worst; it can blow no harder," and then there is a blast ten times more fierce than any before it. So, it was in the compound as the jets screeched overhead and began percussion bombing that sent out tiny shards of metal to inflict painful death on people as a warning that you do not take a stand against America, a nation that decries terror from adversaries while using it themselves.

There were no stouter hearts in the whole world than the hearts of the brave Lakota, and suddenly, also streaking overhead was the newly minted

Lakota Air Force, and though no match in skill to the American pilots, they did outnumber them at least five to one and the Americans broke off the engagement as they waited for reinforcements, while just for good measure, the Lakota sent three planes streaking toward Mount Rushmore, where they first levelled the monument to Lincoln, who had ordered the greatest mass hanging of Native Americans in history, obliterating his head as the pilots cheered in grand elation. It was the slaveholding George Washington who had said, "Indians and wolves are both beasts of prey, tho' they differ in shape." So, as one of the pilots let loose with a missile that cut off the top of his stone head, he let out a war cry and banked left and tipped his wing in salute when another pilot decided to repay Thomas Jefferson for saying, "If ever we are constrained to lift the hatchet against any tribe, we will never lay it down till that tribe is exterminated, or is grandly driven beyond the Mississippi. In war, they will kill some of us; we shall destroy them all." Jefferson's stone carving tumbled down the side of the mountain as cannon fire obliterated the monument to another who had deemed the Native American an affront to white superiority. Finally, all three jets that were roaring through the skies like fire breathing dragons looking for victims, made one more determined pass, opening up cannon fire simultaneously at the monument to a man who had said, "I don't go so far as to think that the only good Indians are dead

Indians, but I believe nine out of ten are, and I shouldn't like to inquire too closely into the case of the tenth." The Teddy Roosevelt monument slithered down the side of the mountain as the three planes veered off and headed toward Wounded Knee. On the way, they dipped their wings in salute as they screeched by the Crazy Horse Monument.

Back at the Wounded Knee compound, the infantry was pressing forward against the defenders, column upon column, a fatigued-glad world of men, twenty thousand of them, bent on the destruction of a group of people that the American nation had long ago decided were unworthy of respect. The world's greatest genocide by a nation that waved the Bible praising their God, but lived by a hypocritical creed that would make the devil proud was once again ready to massacre those it deemed a plight on humanity.

The compound was under bombardment as the President had ordered that no quarter be given and that all there should be pounded into the earth that they all revered so much. Hope had long ago died on the vine of U.S. government genocide against these noble people. However, on this day, those in the compound, stood defiant against evil, unwilling to surrender. They shook hands and prepared to die. Some of them hugged one another with tears in their eyes but no fear. The few machine guns the native army had were spitting lead furiously, but they were up against soldiers in armour that rejected the bullets, although a few were knocked off their feet, only to rise with a cocky grin of arrogance creasing their lips. The tanks were obliterated by artillery and everybody knew it was futile to expect victory, but still they fought on. The dead bodies piled up as the U.S. Army came on and on and on, and they swarmed and stirred and advanced steadily until they were within 1000 metres of the compound.

Aaron and Mary tended to the wounded as exploding shells fell all about. The ground was now crimson, covered with the blood of the martyred dead, dying and wounded who did not cry out, even in their intense pain, because they had already endured the greatest pain imaginable, the pain inflicted by an evil nation of hypocrites.

However, there was some whining and crying back at the White House where the "baby" President was ranting about why it was taking so long to force a surrender by those who dared stand in defiance of him. Suddenly, as he was once again pounding on the desk, an aide came running in, shouting, "The goddamn heathens just blew up Mount Rushmore."

In a wild, frenzied, frantic rant of displeasure, the President said, "I'm firing every one of you fuckers if I don't get some action, and I mean now!"

How many times can the low-life, self-serving, arrogant, boorish maggots of moribund mayhem bow and scrape before a buffoon who is uncouth, uncaring, unintelligent and unmindful of his incredible propensity for foolish assessments of situations that require calm deliberation? Everyone there was almost to the breaking point after only 15 months of working with the most incredibly inept, incompetent buffoon to ever prop his feet up on a desk in the Oval Office. It was almost beyond human endurance to put up with the cartoonish man-child who had no idea how to handle any difficult situation. All his life he had hired people to handle these types of situations for him, but now he was expected to have some competence, and he simply had no reservoir of knowledge allowing any type of serious, sincere evaluation of situations and how to handle them.

McCarty took a long deep breath and said, "That is one blow for them, one small hollow victory, but it will lose them more supporters than it will gain, because Americans honour, respect and adore the men who are on that mountain. Those are the heroes that we are taught to revere. They have destroyed a symbol of American exceptionalism and they will rue the day they did this despicable act."

WHEN JESUS CAME TO THE BLACK HILLS
TO DO THE GHOST DANCE
WITH THE SPIRIT OF SITTING BULL

Sticking out his lower lip, as it quivered in subconscious fear that he was desperately trying to hide, the President said, "I want those fuckers all killed, wiped off the face of the earth. Send in more troops now. I want every possible infantryman available on that reservation, and I want those goddamn Injuns trampled into that fucking ground they think is so scared. Annihilation I tell you. I want total annihilation."

The words bore into the minds of those there, who had supported a tyrant, but they saw no way out. They had thrown their lot in with a despot, and like so many who dance with the devil, thinking they can change the devil; they wind up being changed by the devil.

CHAPTER 12
NO JUSTICE FOR THE POWERLESS

Deep in the man sits fast his fate
To mould his fortunes, mean or great.
Unknown to Jesus, who inside did not see
Dr. Morrison's turmoil of measure and degree.

His personal vendetta against the President
Festered in the missile silo where he was sent.
He worked, plotted and fought demonic affairs,
Against the evil that to no one else compares.

Morrison learned, through doubt and fear,
That in this President evil had no peer.
Obeying time, the last to own
Deep in the earth he sat on his dark throne.

J. Wayne Frye

WHEN JESUS CAME TO THE BLACK HILLS
TO DO THE GHOST DANCE
WITH THE SPIRIT OF SITTING BULL

For Morrison with Jesus was allied,
But Jesus knew not the hatred he signified.
Oh say ye scribes, the foresight that awaits
Is the same genius who revenge creates.

Seemingly, innocuous events dictate many fates, and a faithful day in 1961, Myron Morrison, little boy of 12, wandered into a swampy area about 10 kilometres from his home in Goldsboro, North Carolina and found the resting place of a lost atomic bomb which was the beginning of his desire to be a scientist. For some unknown reason, even he could not fathom at the time, he never revealed the bomb's location.

He studied diligently over the years, determined to become an expert on atomic bombs, and by 25 had his Ph.D. and was recruited by a vast array of defence contractors whose bottom line depended on how many wars could be promoted in the most war-like nation since Hitler came to power in Germany. This American nation had been at near constant war somewhere in the world since it was birthed by a pack of wealthy slave-holding hypocritical businessmen as a way to avoid paying taxes to England. The founders never believed in the phrase "all men are created equal," but simply saw it, like the modern day purveyors of deceit do, as a marketing tool to rally the mindless masses. Patriotism is the refuge of scoundrels in far too many instances, as the privileged class sees it as a way to convince people to become cannon fodder for hypocrisy.

As time passed, Morrison became obsessed with locating other atomic bombs that had been lost during the ludicrous Cold War that had been used by the U.S. government and corporations to excuse the lack of commitment to social justice in order to promote the idea of huge defence expenditures to protect that grand American freedom from those evil, godless commies who were hiding under every bed ready to turn everyone into mindless, robotic socialists. This obsession had nearly broken a nation that fell behind the rest of the First World in providing social amenities to its citizens.

Morrison, through astute research, found the bomb that had been lost in 1958 deep in Georgia's Wassaw Sound on a sand bar at the mouth of the Wilmington River. He kept the two bombs locations secret for over fifty years until he met a charismatic man named Jesus when he was conducting tests on Sioux radiation poisoning at the Canadian Lakota Saskatchewan Reserve.

Recognizing Morrison as a man who had grown weary of the deceit used by the U.S. government, Jesus saw him as someone who might be useful in helping reason with an intractable nation. Having access to the bombs, and making them deliverable above rockets could be used as blackmail against the evil of a government that only understood strength from its foes.

In the dank surroundings deep below ground in one of the two missile silos on Robert Soaring Eagle's farm, Dr. Myron Morrison was in deep thought. He had worked diligently for four years to make two atomic bombs operational while also, with the help of loyal companions, slowly and methodically refurbishing two decommissioned giant Honest John SS-25 rockets in the silos on Robert Soaring Eagle's farm.

As a recognized nuclear radiation genius, Dr. Morrison had earned a great deal of money working in the private sector, and in the early 1980's he lent an immense amount of that money to his father who became a partner in a pipeline that was built by the current President when he was a supposedly a very successful businessman. However, it only took about two years for both Myron Morrison and his father to realize that, like other investors, they had been conned by a man who made an art of filing bankruptcy while using his recognizable name to attract investors. He never really put up any money himself. In the process, he got a large royalty fee for his name, refused to pay vendors and pocketed huge amounts of cash while laundering money for the mob. This was the pattern he had followed ever since inheriting a huge sum of money from his father, a father who saw him as the failure he was and constantly bailed him out of hot water.

This con man broke Morrison and his father, and Morrison's father was so distraught that he committed suicide. The grudge that Dr. Morrison carried was like a slow burning fuse sizzling very deliberately toward a cache of dynamite. He had waited all these years to find someone, somewhere, who somehow might aid him in bringing down this bragging, bombastic buffoon of chicanery.

Jesus was usually a good judge of character, but in his haste to have an ace-in-the-hole against the American government, he did not properly vet Dr. Morrison. He was impressed with what appeared to be his genuine concern about the Saskatchewan Lakota, many of whom had contracted radiation poisoning from the fouled water of the Souris River as a result of mercury being dumped into it from a nuclear power plant on the American side. Thus, Jesus became an unwitting enabler in Morrison's scheme to wreck revenge on a man whom he saw as the murderer of his father.

One night as they sat by a roaring fire and Jesus talked about the plight of the people at the Black Hills Reservation, Dr. Myron Morrison seemed immensely intrigued. He said, "I have heard your plans, and they are safe with me. I have no loyalty to a nation that has the means to do great things, but prefers to spend money on the military rather than on social programmes. It will be difficult finding anyone as disastrous as George Bush was. However, Americans, for an unfathomable reason actually prefer an un-read, un-couth, un-inspiring buffoon as their leader. That old saying that you should never underestimate the stupidity of the American voter is certainly apropos. Of course, the voter is always only given a choice between the lesser of two evils. My guess is the Republicans will find a person with the I.Q. of a flea down the road and he will be elected." (Little did they know at the time that the anti-democratic Electoral College way of choosing the President would hand that office to the biggest buffoon to ever call the White House home.)

They shared a robust round of laughter, and then Morrison said, "Wouldn't it be great if when you try to foment rebellion in the Black Hills you had a real ace in the hole?"

"What do you mean," asked Jesus.

"I can locate and disassemble two nuclear bombs, surreptitiously transport them to two abandoned silos left over from when the Cold War ended. In those silos are the remnants of Honest John rockets. I can reassemble the bombs and the rockets and you have a very big bargaining chip when you negotiate with the government."

Thus, on that night nearly five years before, a plot was hatched by the two men to use a nuclear threat of annihilation to assure the Lakota that they would be able to protect forever their sacred Black Hills. This seemed plausible at the time, but Jesus did not know of the grudge against the President that had been carried deep within Morrison's psyche for so long.

There is great power in numbers, and the current President knew that if he could get the poor and middle class to blame their plight on immigrants, persons of colour, non-Christians and those lazy people who are on welfare, they would willingly support a con-man for President. Yes, convince the people it is the lowly black or brown ghetto dweller who is living lavishly on the overly generous welfare, while the real welfare cheats are the corporations and the wealthy that are the biggest recipients of most government largesse.

If gullibility was an asset, all Americans would be immensely wealthy, because they have a generous supply of it and the trough from which they drink is poisoned with falsehoods to keep them voting against their own interests. The USA is filled with the most easily manipulated people in the world, who are more interested in who won

American Idol than who is stealing their freedom. Ignorance is bliss to the unthinking.

In a country where the exploited will not take off their patriotic blinders in obscene obedience to the 2nd Amendment, there seems to be no hope to change things. These are the very people who actually believe their right to walk around with an AK-47 supersedes the rights of young school children not to face mass slaughter by deranged individuals with easy access to high-powered military weapons. This is the mindlessness of Americans who live in a fantasy world where they actually believe the rest of the world envies them. The delusional white people's adherence to this belief has trapped the uniformed, the ignorant, the prejudiced and the manipulated in permanent subservience to the tyrannical moneyed class that rules with total impunity.

The capitalist class knows no shame in its hypocritical manipulation of the uniformed who believe all their problems stem from the fact that non-whites are on a welfare gravy train that is rolling over the hard steel rails laid by hard-working whites who see themselves as supporters of the lazy idle loafers who are somehow stealing all their money to live a lavish life of leisure. This was what kept the poor whites themselves enslaved, being unable to see who the real culprits of their misery were.

WHEN JESUS CAME TO THE BLACK HILLS
TO DO THE GHOST DANCE
WITH THE SPIRIT OF SITTING BULL

The vast entertainment and news empires in the hands of five or six giant corporations were willing partners in this deception. People were occupied with banal entertainment that turned their minds to mush as it became more important what media whores on reality television ,with their lavish living, were up to than how many children went to bed hungry at night in the richest country in the world. Sports figures prancing like peacocks and music stars that had to parade around nearly naked or engage in elaborate staged displays to hide their lack of real talent were worshipped as if they were really offering something positive to humankind. Thus was the world of American culture that had spread like a cancer all over the earth, causing malignancies of the spirit.

Jesus knew that victory against the despots of capitalism required more than marching, boycotting and begging for your rights. People erroneously assume that you can win fairness from a system that, at its core, is based on unfairness. Workers are simply assets that are to be used, abused and discarded. This process had been in continuous use since creatures crawled out of the sea and evolved into humankind. Through it all, the powerless disenfranchised poor were kept down as a result of a system that enshrined hereditary privilege as a ticket to success, but also as a result of complacency by those who were exploited. This complacency is like a cancer that grows slowly, as after awhile, the people simply accept their fate, as the Lakota had done, with the realization that there is simply nothing that can be done, because no one with power cares. There simply is no justice for the powerless.

CHAPTER 13
DEPTH OF DEPRAVITY

*Let a great assembly be
Of the fearless, of the free,
On some spot of hallowed ground,
Where the plains stretch wide around.*

*Let the blue sky overhead,
The green earth, on which ye tread,
All that must eternal be,
Witness the solemnity.*

*From America's corners uttermost
Of the bounds from coast to coast;
From every city, village and town,
Let the trumpet of freedom sound.*

WHEN JESUS CAME TO THE BLACK HILLS
TO DO THE GHOST DANCE
WITH THE SPIRIT OF SITTING BULL

From the workplace and the prison,
The people exploited are risen,
Women, children, young, and old,
Throw off pain and become bold.

From the haunts of daily life,
Where is waged the daily strife,
People are rising up against greed,
As Jesus has planted freedom's seed.

From the palaces of excess
Heard is the murmur of distress
That echoes like a distant sound
Of a wind alive all around.

Those opulent halls of wealth and fashion,
Where no soul feels any compassion
For those who groan, and toil, and wait,
Now are about to meet their fate.

Arise those who suffer woes untold,
For there is much to feel and to behold.
Your lost country was bought and sold
With a price of the poor's blood and gold.

Let glory from above be,
As all rise from bended knee.
Declare with measured words, that ye
Are finally going to be free.

Be your strong and simple words

J. Wayne Frye 272

WHEN JESUS CAME TO THE BLACK HILLS
TO DO THE GHOST DANCE
WITH THE SPIRIT OF SITTING BULL

Keen to wound as sharpened swords,
And wide as targets of wealth you see.
Slay the privileged class before ye!

Let the tyrants pour around
With a quick and startling sound,
Like the loosening of a sea,
Troops of armed emblazonry.

Let the charged artillery drive,
Till the dead air seems alive
With the clash of clanging wheels,
And the tramp of tyranny under heels.

Stand proud Lakota calm and resolute,
Like a forest close and mute,
With looks of defiance which are
As bright as a shining star.

Let the ancestors of your own land,
Good of will, in sky above stand,
Hand to hand, and foot to foot,
As to the sword your enemies you put.

The shells continued to rain down upon the Lakota. They saw from the plain before them that a tremendous host was moving against their lines. The infantry was pressing on against them, column upon column, a khaki-glad world of men in service to the bankrupt idea of greed, twenty thousand of them. There was no hope at all. They

J. Wayne Frye 273

shook hands, some of them. They nodded boldly to one another with acceptance of their fates. The few did their best. But, everybody knew it was of no use. The dead bodies lay all about. Strangely, no one was praying to the alien Christian God they had been forced to accept. They were real Lakota now, and the white men among them had become in their minds Lakota too.

One Lakota youth took aim at the advancing soldiers and was told by his colleague, "Aim for the head, these soldiers are protected by armour. These are not warriors; they are modern day Pharisees who prance about in arrogant disregard for the code of the warrior. They are no different than the soldiers we faced so very long ago. They are absolutely devoid of honour, as they have been thoroughly brainwashed into believing any cause they engage in is righteous, because they are Americans."

With irreverence for those who did the dirty work of the privileged class, the young warrior took aim and fired, splitting the skull and scattering the propagandized brains of a man who was not a victim of a bullet, but the victim of misplaced loyalty in a nation that saw him as worthy to serve it while the sons and daughters of the wealthy took a pass. The poor had always been cannon fodder for the privileged class, and they simply swallowed the propaganda and lined up for their own slavery. They are always told what a worthy cause they are serving, but the truth is that they are only serving the privileged. One day, perhaps these easily manipulated patriots will say to those who order them into battle, "If it is such a worthy cause, then send your sons and daughters to fight. I'll give them my gun."

As Aaron watched the brave warriors fall, he was transported back to Vietnam in his mind to a time when he first began to see the truth about America and its penchant for enslaving the entire world to its bankrupt capitalistic ideals. He remembered, and he could not think why, a restaurant in Saigon where he had eaten eccentric dishes. Through forced religion, South Vietnam had embraced Catholicism and on all the plates in this unusual restaurant were intricately painted angels.

Aaron wondered why he remembered that oddity in all the misery that lay before him, but there it was. The proprietor had said that he had the plates painted because he had a revelation. The revelation involved a giant cadre of angels ascending from heaven to slay the North Vietnamese Army regulars and their Viet Cong supporters. Aaron laughed at him, because he knew there were no angels, no Jesus, no God. The misery of the world proved that to him. He saw first hand there in the Vietnamese jungles, and then, upon his return, with a Top Secret security clearance at the Pentagon, how America was the biggest terrorist nation in a world dedicated to the enslavement of all humanity to the evil of an obscene economic system. However, on this day the thought of angels would again enter into the mind of this non-believer. Something strange was about to happen, so strange that a logical explanation would be beyond comprehension.

While the battle was raging in the Black Hills, back in the White House, the somewhat sane there in the Oval Office were trying to restrain a steadily mentally unravelling President. His obvious mental ineptitude had been held in restraint since the inauguration, but now the pressure of the moment was wearing down his already flawed and fragile psyche. This was a man on the edge. Those there began to ask themselves how they had stood by this obvious psychopath all this time without exposing his deteriorating mental state that was about to explode in an orgy of uncontrollable mayhem as he edged ever closer to doing the unthinkable.

McCarty was a man of arrogance who saw no deed too despicable in defence of his country. He had supported degradation of prisoners in Afghanistan and Iraq, overt torture at Guantanamo, indiscriminate bombing of women and children in the name of bringing freedom that was nothing more than an elaborate hoax used to secure yet another outpost for American corporate capitalism, but he drew the line at the use of atomic weapons. It was not because he believed them an abomination, but because he believed their use would be detrimental to the long-range plans for American dominance of the world. He knew that the man before him was not beyond any cruel act to satisfy his own hunger for power and revenge against anyone or anything that stood in his way, stood against his need for self-aggrandizement. He was worried that the President was finally unravelling so completely that he would unleash Armageddon.

Back at the compound, where preparations for hand-to-hand combat with the oncoming army were being made, through it all, Jesus did not take up any arms, but moved without fear among the people, urging them to not quit the battle, uttering an invocation that rallied the Lakota patriots as if an electric shock passed through their bodies.

The roar of the battle died down slightly to a gentle murmur as the assault slowed. Still artillery rounds, although fewer, pounded the area. It was then that Jesus, seeing all the suffering about him started to cry, tears flowing like rain down his cheeks. The woman, whose son was the first one to die in this war for justice, moved to him, and gently wiped his cheeks.

WHEN JESUS CAME TO THE BLACK HILLS TO DO THE GHOST DANCE WITH THE SPIRIT OF SITTING BULL

As she wiped the tears away with a coarse cloth she had in her hands, an artillery round landed to her left. She was torn to shreds, her body parts flying all about, but not even a bruise did Jesus receive, as it seemed there was a shield around him, a shield that completely protected him from any harm. Tears again flowed from his eyes as he moved to the centre of the compound and lifted his arms to the heavens as shock and shell fell all about him, the dust of the area rising almost as a whirlwind, but again, not one scratch did he receive as he shouted to the heavens, "enough, enough" and the earth began to shake and rumble so profoundly that it was rippling all the way to the Crazy Horse Monument in Custer County, and the ground beneath the monument also violently shook and slowly the carved face of the mighty Crazy Horse morphed into life as stone became flesh and blood. The unfinished part of the monument, the horse upon which Crazy Horse was to sit, took on form and became flesh also. The people there fell to the ground in shock as the huge horse and rider galloped into the sky, heading in the direction of Wounded Knee. As they looked upward, out of a cloudbank, Crazy Horse was joined in the sky by another figure on a white horse. His long war bonnet flowed majestically down his side, and Chief Crazy Horse had Chief Sitting Bull by his side again, ready to gallop into battle once more and take on the vaunted and widely praised 7th U.S. Air Cavalry.

WHEN JESUS CAME TO THE BLACK HILLS
TO DO THE GHOST DANCE
WITH THE SPIRIT OF SITTING BULL

In the blink of an eye, these two great warriors were galloping in the sky above the hills behind the compound and with them were thousands of warriors. They all wore war paint that glistened like fire in the rays of the sun. The images were so over-powering that even the attacking army stopped its assault and gazed in amazement as their commanders shouted, "Forward men, forward to victory against heathens."

Mary, with Aaron by her side shouted, "TuŋwÁŋ! Itancan!"

Aaron turned to her with a quizzical look and she excitedly said, "TuŋwÁŋ! Itancan! Look at the chiefs! It is Chief Sitting Bull and Chief Crazy Horse."

Aaron's heart grew hot as a burning coal; then it grew cold as ice within him, as in it a tumult of righteous indignation from above answered Jesus' summons.

It was then that the entire Black Hills shook as if an earthquake had rumbled down from the sky rather than the earth, and only one word was uttered. "ThakpÁ!" (Attack!)

At the front was Chief Sitting Bull on a white horse. He did not carry a gun, but had a drawn bow and his war bonnet was as a kingly crown, and he had the countenance of a conqueror bent on revenge for every wrong suffered by his people.

Crazy Horse sat upon a red horse that seemed to spit fire from its nostrils as if was a dragon without wings. To his right was a tall chief on a black horse with a war bonnet almost as long as Sitting Bull's. Someone shouted, "By Crazy Horse's side, it is Chief Gaul."

And to Gaul's right there was a dark-looking chief on a pale horse! Its rider looked like death, as even his war bonnet had only black feathers. He too had his bow quivered with an arrow that was as dark as a night in hell. Someone shouted, "It is Two Moon, the Lakota angel of death rides on our side!"

Thousands of ghostly riders behind the four broke out of formation and galloped all about the assaulting army below just as hundreds of trucks and cars pulled up on the roadways above Crestview Butte which had not been cordoned off by the troops, as their arrogance assumed no one would lend assistance. Out of those vehicles piled armed natives from the nearby Cheyenne, Chippewa and Cree tribes and on the way to Wounded Knee were natives from tribes in Wyoming, Montana, Colorado, New Mexico, Arizona and California – tribes from all across America that had suddenly found the courage to unite against the white man's culture of greed. Also, on the roads into South Dakota were cars, trucks and buses filled with just ordinary Americans who decided to take a stand for justice against their own government that had become an alien power. An incredible uprising was swelling among the forgotten people of America, who had grown weary of rule by the wealthy elite. They were now ready to go to war with those who had stolen their freedom.

All those at sacred Wounded Knee watched in disbelief, as the long line of native warriors in the sky with a giant halo shining about them drew their ancient bows. Suddenly, their cloud of arrows flew singing and tingling through the air towards the 7th, and all the American soldiers laughed that whatever these apparitions were they actually thought the arrows could pierce their armoured plated body coverings.

In unison, all about the Valley of Wounded Knee shouted a frenzied great war cry as the arrows flew. "Sitting Bull, Crazy Horse, slay our enemies!"

The arrows were not made of wood, but of the indignation of a people who had suffered too long the misery promulgated by an alien power in their scared land. Thus, the arrows of indignation ripped through the soldiers' armour. They fell by the hundreds, as the archers quivered their bows again, unleashing more fury on the evil that was there before them.

Meantime, those in the compound were firing all the while. They now had hope; and they aimed with determination to support the warriors in the sky. Suddenly one of them lifted up his voice skyward in the plainest English, "Sitting Bull, Crazy Horse, destroy our enemies!"

A long line of shapes, with radiance about them, drew their bows again, and another volley, a virtual cloud of arrows flew singing and tingling through the air towards the soldiers. The soldiers fell by the hundreds as the arrows pierced their bulletproof vests as if they were hot knives cutting through butter.

Those in the compound and even the advancing army before them gulped with astonishment as the American soldiers were falling by the hundreds. Line after line crashed to the earth in the throes of surprised death as the singing arrows fled so swift and thick that the sun was blotted out, while the patriotically hypnotized horde melted before the ghost warriors.

The American officers leading the charge of evil gulped with astonishment as they heard the guttural screams of their dying men. Still, the singing arrows flew swift and thick as they darkened the sky while the arrogant, bombastic horde of brainwashed robot-like soldiers fell ingloriously upon the sacred ground.

Iudas, showing great fear, was standing by Jesus. As Aaron and Mary rushed to Jesus' side in amazement, Jesus smiled at them and then turned to Iudas while saying to Aaron, "Do you know what the word Iudas translates to from Latin to English?"

"No," retorted Aaron.

"It means Judas, my dear friend," replied Jesus as he stared at Iudas, who was shaking with concern now.

"You shall not kiss my cheek this time, traitor. You told the generals where all our gun emplacements were, so their aim was precise and knocked out our most important assets, but they did not contemplate my call to an army from the sky. Go, and tell those out there that they will all die before my mighty army that I have called from the spirit world to redeem the honour of these noble people. They will pause for now, but they can be called again to lay low the evil that is before us."

"I will be killed," shouted Iudas.

WHEN JESUS CAME TO THE BLACK HILLS
TO DO THE GHOST DANCE
WITH THE SPIRIT OF SITTING BULL

Jesus took a white scarf from a dead body, and staring at Iudas with deep piercing dagger-like eyes, handed it to him and said, "Wave it boldly, and tell what army is left that our ghost warriors will completely annihilate them all if they do not surrender."

General Dumbarton wistfully looked at the table-like buttes surrounding Wounded Knee where thousands of Native Americans had assembled with drawn rifles and were now firing at the advancing soldiers. He could order a strike from the air and obliterate them in the blink of an eye.

Dumbarton was the typical arrogant American general, and the thought of defeat was completely alien to his warped, sadistic mind that like so many of his kind, was imbued with the idea of American invincibility. Then, he gazed through his binoculars with astounding amazement at thousands of his men lying on the ground with arrows piercing through their armoured chests. He looked to the sky and saw the ghost army that was just hovering now above the Wounded Knee compound. He shouted to his aide, "Order the artillery to fire at whatever that illusion is they are projecting in the sky."

A volley of concentrated firepower soared toward the ghost army, but the shells did not pierce what seemed a completely impenetrable shield surrounding the undulating warriors in the sky.

As those shells fell toward the ground, underneath them was the traitor, Iudas, walking with a white flag waving in the dusty air. One shell fell before him and the shards of metal used to instil fear in America's enemies cut him into small pieces and his blood seeped into the ground as his flesh became part of the Black Hills that he had betrayed.

Dumbarton made a direct call to the Command Centre in the Oval office, pleading for help. "We are up against something that is unexplainable. There are fucking ghost warriors in the skies. Rifle wielding natives on the buttes surround us. I have lost thousands of men. They have a damn air force and there are reports of the roadways into Wounded Knee being choked with cars heading this way with armed civilians ready to join these rebellious cretins."

The President was displaying an outward sign of belligerent arrogance, but within this man-child was shivering with fear and doubt. He knew deep within his limitations, which he had covered up with arrogant braggadocio. He began to quiver and his double chin beaded up with sweat as all there were about to see that they had pledged loyalty to a man who knew no restraint when it came to his depth of depravity.

CHAPTER 14
TOWARD HIS DESTINY

Birds find rest in narrow nest,
When-weary of the winged quest;
Beasts find fare in woody lair,
When storm and snow are in the air.

What art thou, freedom? Oh! Could slaves
Answer from their mouldering graves?
This Anarchy a tyrant may fearfully flee
Like a dream's dark and ominous imagery.

Thou art an evil man, as scribes say,
A shadow soon to crawl away,
An abomination of privilege, and a name
Echoing from the eaves of imagined fame.

J. Wayne Frye   287

WHEN JESUS CAME TO THE BLACK HILLS
TO DO THE GHOST DANCE
WITH THE SPIRIT OF SITTING BULL

The labourer for your pleasure you think is bred,
To bow and scrape before a comely table spread.
Thou art in fine clothes devouring the finest food,
While laughing as you trample the multitude.

To the poor thou art an evil wreck
With foot on each and every neck.
From these victims piles of money you make,
While spreading your evil like a slithering snake.

You sit in a White House in D.C.
The blind supporter your evil to never see,
For they adore everything you say,
Without realizing, they too are your prey.

Ah, but there is one with patience and gentleness
That heaven above shines its rays upon to bless.
However, he can also wield a sword.
Anarchy has become Lakota saviour and Lord!

There were no stouter hearts in the whole world than the hearts of the brave men and women at Wounded Knee and on the buttes above the battlefield. These were now the modern descendants of the great warriors who had fought so valiantly against the greatest genocide ever perpetrated against a people.

The remaining American soldiers were trembling with trepidation, as they observed the hovering ghostly army from which they knew there was no escape. Suddenly, this army of evil was overcome with the realization that they were on the wrong side of history. In a fit of recognition that they had been lied to, been brainwashed with patriotic babble and made instruments to serve corporations and the wealthy, they threw down their arms and all raised their hands, except for a few officers who threatened to shoot the mutinying soldiers. These officers were quickly disarmed by their own men. They were stripped of their weapons and as those in the compound and the buttes above shouted their approval, the officers with stooped shoulders began to walk back toward the command post, thoroughly defeated by not only a Native American army, but by their own indignant army that had finally seen the light and joined the side representing justice.

The ghost riders in the sky turned their mounts back toward Custer County. Galloping away there came a cleansing rain as all there on the battlefield felt a calm hush permeate the plains. They had seen the vision clear and plain and even Dumbarton, now a defeated man fleeing in a half-track with his tail between his legs, knew that his time had come and gone. That there was no hope left for him and an army representing greed, because he had received word of troops all over America refusing to go into the cities and quell the marchers demanding an end to tyrannical government in service to the rich.

WHEN JESUS CAME TO THE BLACK HILLS
TO DO THE GHOST DANCE
WITH THE SPIRIT OF SITTING BULL

In hushed silence, all there observed Sitting Bull pull back on his horse's reins and turn his mount back toward the compound as the other ghost riders continued onward. He descended from the sky in a steady gallop, his horse hovering above the church steeple. He waved his hand over the steeple and it tumbled to the ground as if he was saying to all there to turn from the white man's God and embrace their old ways.

Jesus stood before the church smiling and in a slow, methodically smooth motion he waved his right hand from left to right as if to signal to the ghost rider in the sky that his people would honour his request. Sitting Bull turned, his long war bonnet flowing down his back like a string of hope and galloped off into the sky, slowly disappearing from view.

Jesus knew that there was no mystical God up in some grand and glorious heaven in the sky, but there was a God in every person if only they would reach within themselves and find him; find the courage to realize that they were captains of their souls and masters of their fates. God was more idea than reality. And on this day, it seemed that many citizens of this broken kingdom had found the courage to simply no longer allow the rich, the privileged, the religious hypocrites of finger-pointing condemnation and false patriots waving their flags to rule with impunity. They had called on that inner God and found the courage to stand up to authority, stand up to the privileged class, stand up to the flag waving moronic sunshine patriots, stand up to the hypocritical religious paragons of virtue. Outnumbered by the throngs of people who had swarmed into the streets, the police simply did not have the numbers to quell those who had finally reached the breaking point. In fact, many members of the police threw their lot in with the demonstrators, refusing to fire on them, disobeying the orders of those who had served the privileged for so long. In a few cases, they even turned their weapons on their bosses, cutting down without remorse those who were instruments of the ruling class.

There was a real revolution of the masses taking hold and in the gated enclaves where the rich lived in luxurious splendour, the common people were tearing down the gates of opulence that walled off the rich in what they thought was safety, marching into their neighbourhoods, destroying their Rolls Royce's, their Lamborghinis, their Ferraris, taking out the costly furniture and burning it in their yards as the rich stood helplessly in fear, watching what made their lives worthwhile go up in the smoke of indignation from those who had finally had enough. Few people were harmed, but the revolting masses made the moneyed oligarchs shake in fear, just as the oligarchs had made those who served them tremble in fear for years. The vast inequity that had taken hold for so long was also being burned on a pyre of righteousness. This was the mass uprising that had been building in the hearts and minds of the people for many years. This was the end for the moneyed class, all started by a humble man on the Lakota Reservation in South Dakota who had used his remarkable powers to summon an army of retribution against a nation that had no moral core.

At the same time, while in city after city people of good conscience took to the streets and overwhelmed the bigots, white supremacists and flag-waving false patriots all across America, on every reservation the cry went up for all Native Americans to stand with their brothers and sisters to resist the tyranny of an alien power. Like the glorious revolution in 1917 Russia, Americans had finally found the courage to bring their oppressors to their knees.

On Wall Street, hordes swept onto the stock exchange floor, destroying everything in sight and forcing the greedy capitalists to flee in terror. Great cheers went up as the tally boards were destroyed and hurled to the floor, as the greatest symbol of greed in the world was now in the hands of the people.

A huge crowd formed outside the White House, and inside all there trembled in fear. They were preparing to flee out the underground tunnel when someone shouted, "There are armed men in the escape tunnel."

McCarty walked into the hallway outside the Oval Office and barked orders to the Marine guards to kill the intruders in the tunnel. Without hesitation, they fired rounds of hot lead into his cold heart.

The President turned and there before him were his Marine bodyguards who had just dispatched General McCarty. He was shivering, crying like a baby, actually dropping to the floor, kicking and screaming, begging for mercy.

The other servants to this man's delirium of narcissistic arrogance were standing in terror before the guards. The guards contemplated what to do for a few seconds, and despite their desire to kill everyone there, they simply took aim at the black box with the nuclear the codes on the desk and blew it to smithereens.

The President was now curled up in a fetal position, kicking and screaming like the child he had always been. His arrogance and narcissism were at an end, as the Marines motioned for some of those cowering in the far side of the room to get the man-baby and try to comfort him, try to prepare him for the public humiliation that was on its way courtesy of the crowd of furious people who had broken through the White House gate.

The President was babbling incomprehensible gibberish as the crowd swarmed into the Oval Office. They grabbed him by his feet and pulled him out as he finally managed some intelligible words, "I am the President."

The person pulling him looked down and said, "Not anymore asshole."

*The old arrogant rulers of America they
Were faced with the dawning of a new day;
As forgotten voices could be
Heard shouting of new liberty.*

*On those who first would violate
Decency in this terrorist state,
Rested the blood that must ensue,
As the natives had gotten their due.*

*And if then the tyrants still dare,
As real Americans ride among them there;
Slash, and stab, and maim, and hew;
Until the evil is slain and left are but a few.*

*With folded arms and steady eyes,
And little fear and less surprise,
Look upon them as they stay
Till their rage has died away.*

J. Wayne Frye   294

WHEN JESUS CAME TO THE BLACK HILLS
TO DO THE GHOST DANCE
WITH THE SPIRIT OF SITTING BULL

Then they will flee with shame,
To the place from which they came,
And the blood thus shed will speak
In hot blushes on each tyrant's cheek.

And that slaughter to this nation
Shall steam up like inspiration,
Eloquent Lakota now shine like a star
And their triumph explodes like a volcano afar.

And the words of freedom shall then
Wash away the oppressive sin,
Ringing through each heart with pride
In the liberty for which Lakota died.

Ye who rose like lions after slumber
In unvanquishable number
Shook your chains to earth like dew,
Now glory and freedom shine on you.

Back at Wounded Knee as news of what was happening all over America reached them, Jesus was standing on a makeshift dais before the crowd. He very humbly said, as he looked down at Aaron, who was standing with Mary right below him, "You have won a great victory today against the evil of greed. All across this nation, you lit a fire that hopefully will not be put out until the last vestige of greed is buried once and for all-time, so that people can reach their full potential unimpeded by social and economic injustice."

J. Wayne Frye   295

He got tears in his eyes as he continued. "My work here is done, for there is still great injustice in other places with the same vile inequities that destroyed the fabric of this nation for so many years. I cannot and will not rest as long as anywhere in the world there is one person suffering from inequity and injustice. I bid you farewell and do not ever let injustice triumph again."

He climbed down from the dais to pleas from the crowd for him to stay, but as he hugged Mary, then Aaron, it was obvious to the two that he had other rebellions to lead in places where injustice and the evil of greed kept humans in chains. They both bid him a fond farewell as he made his way toward the highway, shaking hands and hugging people on the way. He hailed a passing car, crawled into the back and the Son of Anarchy sped away toward his destiny.

WHEN JESUS CAME TO THE BLACK HILLS
TO DO THE GHOST DANCE
WITH THE SPIRIT OF SITTING BULL

EPILOGUE
AS HE THOUGHT

Jesus in triumph stood
Having done all he could
He left word in verse
To those once cursed.

Let the thick curtain fall;
I better know than all
How little I have gained;
How vast the unattained.

Others shall sing the song,
Others shall right the wrong,
Finish what I begin,
And all I failed to win.

J. Wayne Frye   297

WHEN JESUS CAME TO THE BLACK HILLS
TO DO THE GHOST DANCE
WITH THE SPIRIT OF SITTING BULL

What matter, I or they?
Mine or another's day,
So the right word be said
And life the sweeter made?

Hail to the coming singers!
Hail to the brave light-bringers!
Forward I reach and share
All that they sing and dare.

The airs of heaven blow o'er me;
A glory shines before me
Of what mankind shall be,
Pure, generous, brave and free.

Ring bells in un-reared steeples,
The joy of unborn peoples!
Sound, trumpets far off blown,
Your triumph is my own!

Ironically, all the hostages held in the compound survived the intense shelling as the church was spared, perhaps, because the U.S. Army feared the backlash from the Bible thumpers if they levelled a church. It did not matter now, because those same Bible thumpers were about to witness the end of their reign of hypocrisy, as the nation was now in the hands of those dedicated to the strict separation of church and state. It was Lu Ann Luce who looked at Aaron and Mary with intense hatred as she said, "Damn you communists!"

J. Wayne Frye   298

WHEN JESUS CAME TO THE BLACK HILLS
TO DO THE GHOST DANCE
WITH THE SPIRIT OF SITTING BULL

Aaron stared back and said, "No, damn you greedy capitalists who now will face justice."

She took a deep breath and said, "Where's my limousine and driver?"

Aaron took Mary's hand and walked away, knowing that the only way to end the arrogance of the rich and privileged was with a bullet. Would some of the leaders have the courage to stand them all against a wall and end their tyranny? No, because those now seizing power had a conscience, and they could not understand that the tyranny of those who think they are special can only be stopped with a bullet. Was this only temporary respite from the evil of the privileged class?

Aaron looked lovingly at his beloeved Mary and said, "There is one element in all this that still concerns me."

"What is that?" replied Mary.

"There is a man sitting in a missile silo on a farm who is a question mark. He was Jesus' ace-in-the-hole in case all failed. I am not sure he is reliable, and I know where he is. I am certain he has heard what has happened, but I am fearful of what he might do with the destructive power at his disposal. "

Mary said, "The we must go to that farm."

Aaron took her hand and walked toward some nearby cars. They commandeered one and headed north to the farm of Robert Soaring Eagle.

There are strange bedfellows in the pursuit of justice. Although the ultimate aim is to end the tyranny of the wealthy and privileged, the players on the stage of revolution are not all pure of purpose. Myron Morrison was one of those players with questionable motives. His grudge against the President was more personal than philosophical; although he shared the goals of the Lakota people in their pursuit of justice. Still, as he sat by his desk looking at the two assistants who were ready to take the elevator up and leave the darkness of the launch bunker, he refused to leave with them, saying that he would wait for final word from Jesus.

The assistants left, and there alone, Morrison studied and thought for a good half hour as he looked over at the button that would light the fuel in the rockets and prepare them for launch. He thought of all the innocents who would suffer as the two warheads exploded over the White House and the Pentagon. Millions would die for no reason, as the goals of the revolt had been achieved beyond the original intent. He even knew his primary personal goal of deposing the

President was, no doubt, achieved. Yet, within him hatred seethed.

He pushed the button that lit the solid rocket fuel and eased back in his chair. Staring at the green launch button, he took a deep breath and thought about what he should do? The man who was responsible for his father's death was still in the White House, or at least still in Washington, and he deserved death for all his many transgressions.

As Mary and Aaron frantically sped toward the farm, Dr. Myron Morrison slowly moved his finger toward that green button as he thought and thought and thought..

*Don't Miss These Other
Aaron Adams Adventures
By J. Wayne Frye
From*
Fireside Books
*Something Evil in the Darkness at Hopkins House
When Jesus Came to Jersey as the Son of Thunder
White Meteors and the Ghost of Sue Ann McGee
The Girl Who Said Goodbye for the Last Time
The Girl Who Motivated Murder Most Foul
The Girl Who Stirred up the Whirlwind
When Jesus Came to Canada
Fall From Apocalypse
The Disappearance
Armageddon Now*